Ev... ...s she
fou... ...crisp
dark bro...
shaped ...
frami... ...
his jaw...

Her ga... ...
well-musc...
cut high at t...
showing off w...
looked fit and h...
jaundiced eyes, th... ...ipped.

She didn't need this! She had allowed physical attraction to dictate her actions once before and look how that had ended—with her life in tatters and her spirit shattered. All she wanted now was to pick up the threads and weave them together, attempt to get back what she had lost and by doing so find herself. No matter how attractive Ryan was she wasn't going to get involved with him. *Ever.*

She glanced deliberately at her watch and shrugged. 'Is that the time? I'll have to go.'

'Me too.'

He treated her to one of his wonderfully warm smiles and Eve had to force herself not to respond. There was no point encouraging him, after all.

'See you tomorrow,' she called, hurrying away.

She rounded a bend in the path and slowed, aware that her heart was racing. The one thing she had never allowed for was that she would be attracted to another man, but there was no point denying it. She was attracted to Ryan and she had to keep well away from him…

She groaned when it struck her how difficult it was going to be. Avoiding Ryan wasn't possible when they had to work together, but somehow she had to keep a rein on her feelings. The thing she mustn't do was make another mistake.

Dear Reader

I had wanted to write this story for some time, but I just couldn't seem to find the right characters who would be able to handle such an emotive tale. Then one day, when I was out walking my dog, Eve and Ryan suddenly appeared in my head and I knew they would be perfect.

They both have major issues to contend with and they have both suffered in the past, making them afraid of what the future holds in store for them. However, when they meet up again and start to fall in love, they realise that they can help one another if they are willing to take a chance.

I really loved writing this book. Eve and Ryan are two brave people who deserve to find happiness. If you would like to know more about the background to this book then do visit my blog: Jennifertaylorauthor.wordpress.com. I would love to hear your comments.

Love

Jennifer

MR RIGHT ALL ALONG

BY
JENNIFER TAYLOR

Published in Great Britain 2014
by Mills & Boon, an imprint of Harlequin (UK) Limited,
Eton House, 18-24 Paradise Road, Richmond, Surrey, TW9 1SR

© 2014 Jennifer Taylor

ISBN: 978 0 263 90741 4

Harlequin (UK) Limited's policy is to use papers that are natural,
renewable and recyclable products and made from wood grown in
sustainable forests. The logging and manufacturing processes conform
to the legal environmental regulations of the country of origin.

Printed and bound in Spain
by Blackprint CPI, Barcelona

Jennifer Taylor lives in the north-west of England, in a small village surrounded by some really beautiful countryside. She has written for several different Mills & Boon® series in the past, but it wasn't until she read her first Medical Romance™ that she truly found her niche. She was so captivated by these heart-warming stories that she set out to write them herself! When she's not writing, or doing research for her latest book, Jennifer's hobbies include reading, gardening, travel, and chatting to friends both on and off-line. She is always delighted to hear from readers, so do visit her website at www.jennifer-taylor.com

Recent titles by Jennifer Taylor:

THE MOTHERHOOD MIX-UP
THE REBEL WHO LOVED HER†
THE SON THAT CHANGED HIS LIFE†
THE FAMILY WHO MADE HIM WHOLE†
GINA'S LITTLE SECRET
SMALL TOWN MARRIAGE MIRACLE
THE MIDWIFE'S CHRISTMAS MIRACLE
THE DOCTOR'S BABY BOMBSHELL*
THE GP'S MEANT-TO-BE BRIDE*
MARRYING THE RUNAWAY BRIDE*
THE SURGEON'S FATHERHOOD SURPRISE**

†*Bride's Bay Surgery*
*Dalverston Weddings
**Brides of Penhally Bay

**These books are also available in eBook format
from www.millsandboon.co.uk**

To my nephews, Neil and Simon Burgess, who undertook the Three Peaks Challenge and not only raised a lot of money for charity but also saved their poor aunt from having to do it in the name of research!

Thanks, boys. You are both stars!

CHAPTER ONE

'BAA, BAA, BLACK *sheep have you any wool? Yes, sir, yes, sir, three bags full.*'

Ryan Sullivan winced as he passed the door to Dalverston General's High Dependency Paediatric Unit. Whilst he would never have claimed to possess a wonderful singing voice, at least he could carry a tune—which was more than could be said for whoever was murdering that nursery rhyme! He eased open the door, feeling surprise shoot through him when he saw Eve Pascoe sitting beside the bed. Apart from the fact that it was lunchtime and she should be taking her break, Eve was the last person he would have expected to be giving such a rousing performance.

Ryan frowned as that thought sank in. He had first met Eve during his rotations—they'd been students together in London and had trained at the same hospital. Eve had been bright, witty, funny, warm...everything she wasn't any more. What had happened to her in the past few years? he wondered, not for the first time. Why had she changed so much? Although she was always polite whenever he spoke to her, she was so distant these days and not just towards him either.

Eve had been at Dalverston General for almost two months now yet she hadn't made any attempt to join in the usual extramural staff activities. Invitations to curry nights and cinema trips had been politely refused without any reason being given. She had earned herself a reputation for being a bit of a snob, in fact, although Ryan didn't believe that. Maybe Eve did come from a very wealthy background but he had known her before and there had been nothing snobby about Eve Pascoe then, he recalled, and wondered why the thought disturbed him so much. He might be intrigued to find out what had happened to her, but it was friendly curiosity, that was all. He certainly wasn't *romantically* interested in her.

Eve suddenly looked up and Ryan smoothed his face into a noncommittal expression. He didn't do romance, didn't do commitment, didn't do anything that might cause anyone any grief. Love and all its attendant problems weren't on his agenda now or ever.

'I heard you singing,' he said, returning to what had brought him into the room. He grinned when she blushed. 'It was, well…*different*, shall I say.'

'Daisy's mother said it was her favourite nursery rhyme,' Eve replied defensively, standing up.

She bent over the bed where five-year-old Daisy Martin was lying curled up into a tight little ball and Ryan got another shock when he saw her smile at the child. She looked so like the old Eve when she smiled like that, happy and warm and caring. It made the change in her all the more marked so that his interest was piqued even more. He realised that he wouldn't

rest until he had found out what had happened to bring
about such a massive change in her.

'I'll come back to see you later, sweetheart. Close
your eyes and have a little sleep now. There's a good
girl.' She gently smoothed back the child's thick black
curls then headed to the door, pausing when Ryan
failed to move out of her way.

'Sorry.'

He stepped aside, automatically following her along
the corridor although he had been heading to the can-
teen before he'd got sidetracked. Still, lunch could
wait. He was more interested in finding out what had
happened to Eve in the past few years, although he
wasn't vain enough to think she would simply come
out and tell him. Eve preferred to keep her own coun-
sel these days and she would be as unlikely to open
her heart to him as to anyone else.

The thought stung just a little and far more than
it should have done. Although they'd been friends—
good friends too—they'd not had a relationship; Ryan
had made sure of that. Oh, there'd been that one occasion after he had kissed her under the mistletoe when
he had almost caved in but he had realised in time
what a mistake it would be.

Although Eve was extremely pretty with that long
red-gold hair and those wonderful grey-green eyes,
she was very different from the women he normally
dated. He preferred women who were more worldly
wise, women, like him, who weren't looking for commitment, and Eve hadn't fitted that bill. Even though
she had ticked so many other boxes, he had never tried
to turn their friendship into something more, espe-

cially after that kiss. He had realised that night how easy it would be to get involved with her and it had been the last thing he'd wanted.

It had been a relief, in fact, when she'd started seeing one of the registrars a short time later because it had stopped him fantasising about what might have been. Eve wasn't for him but even though he'd known that, it had been harder than he'd expected to get her out of his head after that kiss. However, once Damien Blackwell had appeared on the scene, everything had changed. Eve's time had been taken up by Damien and she'd stopped spending so much time with him and their friends.

Ryan had told himself he was glad that she was happy, and he had been too even though he had missed her. Their friendship had meant a lot to him so he'd been stunned when he had heard that she had dropped out of the training programme. Eve hadn't told him what she was planning; one day she'd been there and the next she'd gone and that was the last he'd seen of her. Although he had often wondered why she had given up, he hadn't tried to find her. He'd been wary of doing that, of getting involved. He had nothing to offer Eve so he had told himself that it was her decision and that was the end of the matter.

Now, however, Ryan couldn't help wondering if it was Damien who was responsible for the change in her, Damien who had taken away her sparkle, her warmth, her humour and turned her into the distant young woman she was today. He sensed it was true and a rare rush of anger swept through him. He couldn't bear to think that Eve's life had been blighted by the other man. It made his own decision not to get involved all the more valid. *He* didn't intend to be responsible for ruining some poor woman's life!

Eve brought up Daisy Martin's file on the computer. The little girl had sickle cell anaemia, an inherited blood disease. Daisy's red blood cells were abnormal resulting in a chronic and very severe form of anaemia. The youngest of three children born to Jamaican parents, Daisy was the only one to have inherited the condition. It had first presented itself when she'd been a baby, causing fatigue, headaches, shortness of breath and jaundice. Although Daisy had been fairly well for some time, she had recently suffered a crisis and had been admitted to HDPU as she required careful nursing. She was such a lovely child too, Eve thought sadly as she started to write up her notes. It didn't seem fair that she should suffer this way.

She typed in the time and the date, doing her best to ignore Ryan. She always felt uneasy around him, always on her guard, always wary in case she slipped up. After all, Ryan had known her in the old days, pre-Damien, and she was very aware that he must have noticed how much she had changed.

She sighed, recalling her shock when she'd discovered that Ryan was working at Dalverston General. She had applied for the post specifically because she'd thought she would be unlikely to meet up with anyone she had known in the past. Her peers had moved on to bigger and better things and, like Ryan, were part way up the professional ladder now.

Dropping out had set her back and she had a lot of

ground to make up. She didn't need the added stress of having to explain why she had given up her studies. She had explained it all to Roger Hopkins, the hospital's manager, when she had been for her interview, and that had been difficult enough.

Thankfully, it was only Ryan who knew what she had done and although people might wonder why she was still an F1 at her age, it was doubtful if they would ask, especially when she made a point of keeping them at arm's length. If anyone questioned her, it would be Ryan so she had to be especially careful around him. Maybe they had been good friends but she didn't want to admit to him what a fool she'd been and had no intention whatsoever of letting him know how ashamed she felt. She would feel even more humiliated if Ryan found out the truth.

'Daisy's definitely improving, isn't she?'

Ryan sat down on the edge of the desk and Eve flinched. She couldn't help it. Although she had learned to deal with her fear of physical contact with regard to her patients, it still made her feel a little panicky whenever anyone got too close, especially a man.

Not every man was like Damien, she reminded herself. Ryan wasn't a bully or a control freak....or not so far as she knew. He had been warm and funny and full of good humour when she'd known him before and he didn't appear to have changed, although she couldn't be sure, could she? Damien had seemed very different in the beginning, before she had got to know him better and discovered what he was capable of.

Panic rose inside her and she had to breathe in and out before she could reply. Even then her voice sounded strained and she hated it. She didn't want to be like this, didn't want to be a victim, but that's what she was. She had allowed Damien Blackwell to take over her life, to take control of *her*. It would be a long time before she found her true self again, if it ever happened.

'She is. She's a lot brighter today.' Eve quickly typed in the few sentences that were all that were needed to update the file and saved it. Standing up, she came around the desk and had to pause yet again when she realised that she couldn't get past Ryan without touching him. Even though she was over the worst of her fears, the thought of feeling his skin brush against hers made her breath catch. She could cope with touching the children, could even manage to touch another adult if the occasion warranted it, but the thought of touching Ryan made her tremble for some reason.

'Hey, are you all right?' He leant forward, his dark brown eyes filled with concern. 'You've gone really pale. Do you feel faint?'

Eve struggled to get a grip. 'I...I never had any breakfast,' she murmured. Would she ever get over this fear completely, ever be able to enjoy a physical relationship again? She had tried everything, had had counselling, spoken to other victims of abuse, but the fear was so deeply rooted, the memories too clear: first the seemingly loving touch and then the violence...

'Come on. I'll treat you to lunch.'

Ryan put his hand under her arm to lead her to the door and Eve freaked out. She pushed him away.

'Don't touch me!'

He stepped back at once, his face set. 'I'm sorry. I didn't mean to upset you. Maybe you should go and get something to eat. You obviously need it.'

He spun round on his heel and stalked out of the door, making it clear that he was deeply offended. Eve sank down onto a chair, her whole body trembling as reaction set in. What a fool she was! Why on earth had she reacted that way? Now it would be all round the unit that she was unbalanced, unstable...

Only she doubted if Ryan would tell anyone what had happened. From what she remembered, he wasn't like that. He had been kind and supportive when she had known him before and she wanted to believe that *he* hadn't changed even if she had.

Eve took a deep breath, surprised by how important that idea was. Knowing that Ryan hadn't changed made her feel better for some reason.

Ryan found it impossible to put what had happened out of his mind. All through afternoon ward rounds he found himself thinking about the way Eve had reacted when he had touched her. It wasn't the usual response he received: most women were more than happy to have him touch them and a whole lot more. However, there had been genuine fear in Eve's eyes and he could only put it down to one reason: had she been subjected to some sort of physical abuse?

The thought was more than he could stand and he knew that he had to find out the truth. If Eve had been in an abusive relationship, he wanted to help her. If he could. He sighed as he finished explaining to Rex

Manning, their consultant, that he was hoping to discharge the patient they were examining the following day. Why on earth should Eve trust him, after all?

'Good. This is what I like to see, my patients making rapid progress.' Rex smiled charmingly at seven-year-old Alfie Hudson's anxious parents. Alfie had been admitted with appendicitis, which had been successfully dealt with, and Rex was keen to enjoy the kudos even though it was Ryan who had performed the surgery. 'An excellent result, wouldn't you say, Mr and Mrs Hudson?'

Ryan grimaced as the young couple immediately showered Rex with praise. Although Rex was a bit of a diva, he was excellent at his job and Ryan was prepared to cut him a lot of slack because of it. He caught Eve's eye and winked and, amazingly, she winked back. It was such a surprise after her earlier rejection that it felt as though he was floating on air as they proceeded to the next bed, and it was unnerving to realise that she could have this effect on him. Maybe he did want to help her, but he couldn't afford to get too involved in her affairs.

He had his own agenda, things he needed to do, things that were too important to put off. He was the lucky one after all. He was still here, enjoying his life, doing what he wanted. His twin brother, Scott, hadn't been so lucky. Scott hadn't had time to make his mark on the world so he, Ryan, had to do it for him. The fact was that he didn't have time to worry about Eve when he had so much else to focus on.

Ryan knew it was true. It was what he had decided after Scott had died so tragically when they were seventeen. He had sworn then that Scott wouldn't be forgotten and he had worked towards that aim for all these years. It was thanks to his efforts that the money for over thirty portable defibrillators had been raised. They had been placed in shopping centres, swimming pools, sports arenas and the next step was to get them into schools.

No one should die as Scott had done because of a lack of equipment. No parents should have to go through the horror of losing a child as his parents had done. Ryan had set himself this task and he would carry it through to the bitter end, until he was too old to run another sponsored race or climb one more mountain. He didn't have time for a relationship even if it were possible.

He glanced at Eve and felt his heart contract in alarm. He knew what he had to do, so why did it suddenly seem more important that he help Eve, turn her back into the warm and caring woman she had been?

CHAPTER TWO

IT WAS GONE seven before Eve left the hospital. Daisy Martin's parents had asked to speak to her and she had spent some time reassuring them. One of the worst things about sickle cell anaemia was that nobody could predict when a crisis would occur. It made it even more stressful for Daisy's parents.

Evening visiting was under way as she walked through the main doors. She was renting a flat close to the river and she decided to walk home rather than wait for the bus, which would be packed. It was a warm evening, the sun just sliding below the surrounding hills.

Originally, Dalverston had been a sleepy little market town straddling the borders of Lancashire and Cumbria. Although it had expanded in the past thirty years, it had retained its charm and attracted many visitors. With Easter just a week away, there were a lot of tourists in the area and Eve had to wait until the lights changed before she could cross the road. She had always lived in the city before and had wondered if she would adapt to a more rural way of life but it had turned out better than she had expected. She felt safe here, safe and secure, and that was something she valued more than anything.

She reached the footpath leading down to the river and decided to take a short cut. It was quicker this way and she wanted to get home as soon as possible. It had been a difficult day and it would be a relief to go in and shut the door on the world, although she wasn't foolish enough to think she could forget what had happened. She had overreacted when Ryan had touched her and she knew that he must be wondering why she had behaved so oddly. Would he ask her or would he let it pass? It all depended how interested he was in her, she decided.

The thought sent a shiver down her spine and she quickened her pace. She couldn't bear the thought of Ryan finding out what had happened. She felt ashamed enough without people knowing how stupid she had been. She had allowed Damien Blackwell to rule her life because she'd thought he had loved her, but it hadn't been love; it had been something far more destructive. It had taken her a while to realise it and when she had, she'd also realised that she could never trust her own judgement again. She had been taken in once and it could happen a second time.

That bleak thought kept her company as she made her way along the path. It was so peaceful away from the traffic that she felt herself start to relax for the first time since her encounter with Ryan. She *had* overreacted and she really should apologise, but what could she say? That the thought of any man laying his hands on her filled her with horror? That would only give rise to more questions and that was the last thing she wanted. Something told her that she would find it harder to withhold the truth from Ryan than from anyone else.

Ryan felt too restless to spend the evening watching television. What had happened with Eve had continued to trouble him and he found that he couldn't put it out of his mind. He was more convinced than ever that something awful had happened to her and the thought plagued him. Eve had been so sweet and funny and it wasn't right that she should have suffered in any way. He wanted to offer her his support, although he guessed that she would reject it. Eve didn't want anything from him, as she had made clear.

In an effort to take his mind off the subject, he decided to go for a run. He was undertaking the Three Peaks Challenge to raise more funds in a few weeks' time and he needed to step up his training. As soon as he got home, he changed into his running clothes and set off, taking the path that led along the riverbank. It was a mild evening, perfect for running, and he soon found himself unwinding. Maybe there was something he could do to help Eve, he mused. If he could just persuade her to trust him, it would be a start.

He rounded a bend and came to an abrupt halt when he almost cannoned right into Eve. 'Sorry!' he exclaimed, reaching out to steady her when she staggered. His hands gripped her forearms and he felt to the very second when surprise turned to something else. He quickly released her, trying to clamp down on the anger that rose inside him. Nobody should feel this scared, and especially not Eve!

'I...I didn't know you enjoyed running.' Her voice was tight, hinting at the effort it cost her to speak at all, and he was overwhelmed with tenderness. Maybe she was scared but she was doing her best not to show it.

'I'm not sure if I actually enjoy it but it's a necessary evil,' he replied lightly, grinning at her. 'I'm supposed to be doing the Three Peaks Challenge soon and I need to get down to some serious training. I'd hate to think that I'll be the one who has to drop out on the first leg!'

She smiled back. 'I doubt that will happen. You look pretty fit to me.'

It was the sort of throwaway comment that anyone might have made; however, the fact that it was Eve who had made it did all sorts of things to his libido. Ryan cleared his throat, terrified that he would do the unforgivable and let her see the effect it was having on him. Eve hadn't meant anything by it, he told himself sternly. And she certainly hadn't meant to imply that she found him attractive!

'I wish I shared your confidence.' He managed to hold his smile but it was tough. Since he and Eve had met up again he had followed her lead and kept his distance. It was obviously what she wanted yet he couldn't help wondering if he should have been more proactive. If he'd taken a different approach then maybe she would have found it easier to confide in him? The thought spurred him on even though the voice of reason was telling him to back off. He didn't have time to worry about Eve when he had so much else on his agenda, reason insisted, but the advice fell on deaf ears.

'I've become a real couch potato during the winter. I don't think I've been out running more than a handful of times since Christmas, in fact. No way will I manage to climb the three highest mountains in Britain unless I put in some serious work.'

'I see. Are you doing it as personal challenge or for charity?' she queried, pushing back a strand of red-gold hair as the wind whipped it across her face.

'Charity,' Ryan replied thickly. He cleared his throat, doing his utmost to behave sensibly. He liked women and they liked him. He seemed to have a genuine rapport with the opposite sex, in fact, so that he had never really thought about all the nuances of a relationship. If he asked a woman out and she accepted—which she usually did—he simply got on with enjoying her company. If the relationship moved on to something more intimate, that was great. If it didn't then he had made himself another friend.

What he had never done was stand around dissecting his feelings, totting up how much of what he felt was based on sexual attraction. He always saw a woman as a whole person and yet here he was, awash with lust, because he couldn't get past the thought of touching that silky strand of hair!

'I'm raising money to put a couple of portable defibrillators into the local high school,' he explained hastily. Thinking about Scott, and what he needed to do, always focused his mind, although it didn't seem to be quite as effective as usual. He hurried on.

'Once they're sorted, I'll make a start on the primary schools.'

'I see.' Eve frowned, an almost imperceptible puckering of her brow, and his libido took a giant leap and set off running again. 'It's a great idea, obviously, but what made you get involved in a project like that?'

'My brother.' Ryan swallowed but there didn't seem to be even the tiniest drop of moisture in his mouth. He longed to continue, to bombard Eve—and himself—with facts so he could forget how much he would like to smooth away those tiny frown lines, but it wasn't possible.

'He's involved too, is he?'

'In a way, yes.'

'Funny, I never knew that you had a brother.'

Her frown deepened, as well it might, Ryan realised bleakly. Although they had been good friends and swapped a lot of confidences, he had never told her about Scott. They had chatted about work, about their ambitions, about music they liked and films they had seen, but never about the one thing that had had the biggest influence on his life. Now he realised with a start that he hadn't told her because he'd wanted their conversations to be a sort of haven. When he was with Eve, he could forget everything else. He wasn't Scott's brother or his parents' sole remaining child: he was simply himself.

Eve had no idea what was going on inside Ryan's head and she didn't want to know either. Something warned her that it would be far too stressful. She summoned a smile, the sort of brightly meaningless smile she had spent ages practising in front of her bedroom mirror. After she had left Damien, she hadn't smiled for months. There'd been nothing to smile about, but gradually she had realised that she had to play her part for other people's benefit. They would only ask questions if she went around with a long face.

'That's good. It must be nice to share a common interest.'

'It would be if Scott was around.'

Ryan's voice was so empty of emotion that it rang hollowly. Eve's eyes flew to his face and her heart contracted when she saw the expression it held. Even though she really didn't want to ask the question, she had no choice. She couldn't ignore the pain in his eyes, couldn't pretend she didn't see it even though it was what she longed to do.

'What do you mean? Why isn't he around?'

'My brother died when we were seventeen. We were twins—fraternal, not identical. Not that it makes any difference, of course.'

'I had no idea…' She stopped and he shrugged.

'Why should you? I never told you about him so there's no way you could have known.'

'Why?' The word slid out before she could stop it and she bit her lip. She was falling into the trap she'd wanted to avoid, asking questions, listening to answers, moving that bit closer to another human being. She needed to remain detached, indifferent, uninvolved but it wasn't possible. Not with Ryan anyhow.

'Why didn't I tell you?' He grimaced. 'Oh, all sorts of reasons. Because I wanted to enjoy our conversations without having to think about what had happened. Because I didn't want to be Scott's brother, i.e. the twin who *hadn't* died. Because, selfishly, I just wanted to be myself with all that did and didn't entail.'

His honesty affected her far more than it should have done. Eve felt a wave of sympathy wash over her. Reaching out, she went to touch his hand then stopped. Even though she longed to comfort him, she needed to maintain her distance.

'It wasn't selfish. It must have been…well, very hard for you.'

'Not as hard as it was for Scott.' His tone was wry but it didn't conceal the pain he felt and her heart ached all the more.

'I can't begin to imagine what it must be like to lose someone you love, but it wasn't your fault, Ryan. You weren't to blame in any way.'

'I know that.'

He shrugged, his shoulders rising and falling beneath the close-fitting black T-shirt he was wearing, and Eve's heart performed another odd manoeuvre, one it hadn't performed for many years. All of a sudden she was aware of him in a way that she hadn't been since that night when he had kissed her under the mistletoe at the hospital Christmas party. It had started out as a joke. Egged on by their friends, Ryan had rolled his eyes and given in and kissed her. However, the moment his mouth had found hers, everything had changed.

Eve could still recall her shock as wave after wave of sensation had poured through her. Although she'd been kissed before, she had never felt anything like it. Ryan's lips had awoken feelings inside her that she'd never experienced before, made her feel hot and hungry, made her want more than just a kiss. When he had let her go, she'd felt dazed and disorientated, filled with wonder that a mere kiss could arouse such a response inside her. She'd half expected him to do it again, to kiss her in private this time without their friends cheering them on, but he hadn't.

If anything, he had become decidedly distant in the days following—taking his breaks separately from her, turning down invitations for them to have lunch together with the flimsiest of excuses. Eve had felt incredibly hurt at first until she'd realised that he was simply acting true to form. Ryan didn't do relationships, didn't do commitment, didn't do anything that might encourage a woman to think he wanted her in his life long term. Maybe he was happy to have her as a friend but that was all.

Now, however, Eve's eyes widened, her pupils dilating as she found herself taking fresh stock of the crisp dark brown hair clipped close to his well-shaped head, the dark slash of his eyebrows framing equally dark eyes, the firm strength of his jaw. Her gaze swooped lower, running over the broad shoulders, a well-muscled chest, trim waist. He was wearing running shorts cut high at the sides and they made the most of his long legs, showing off well-developed thigh muscles and firm calves. He looked fit and healthy and so incredibly attractive, even to her jaundiced eyes, that she gulped.

She didn't need this! She had allowed physical attraction to dictate her actions once before and look how it had ended, with her life in tatters and her spirit shattered. All she wanted now was to pick up the threads and weave them together, attempt to get back what she had lost and by doing so find herself. No matter how attractive Ryan was, she wasn't going to get involved with him. Ever.

'Good. I'm glad to hear it,' she said in a cool little voice that was totally at odds with how she felt. She glanced deliberately at her watch and shrugged. 'Is that the time? I'll have to go.'

'Me too.' He treated her to one of his wonderfully warm smiles and Eve had to force herself not to respond. There was no point encouraging him, after all.

'See you tomorrow,' she called, hurrying away. She rounded a bend in the path and slowed, aware that her heart was racing. The one thing she had never allowed for was that she would be attracted to another man but there was no point denying it. She was attracted to Ryan and she had to keep well away from him...

She groaned when it struck her how difficult it was going to be. Avoiding Ryan wasn't possible when they had to work together but somehow she had to keep a rein on her feelings. The thing she mustn't do was make another mistake.

Ryan did his best not to think about his encounter with Eve on the riverbank but failed. Miserably. As the week wended its way towards the weekend, he found himself returning to those minutes they had spent together far too often. Maybe Eve hadn't said anything but he'd have needed to be deaf, dumb *and* blind not to have noticed her reaction. She had looked at him and he'd known that it had been a lightbulb moment for her the same as it had been for him. Because if Eve had suddenly realised he was a man, he had definitely realised that she was a woman. A very attractive woman too.

Saturday rolled around and he thanked merciful heaven that he didn't have to go into work. He had the weekend off, forty-eight hours completely Eve-free. If he didn't manage to sort himself out then it wouldn't be for want of trying, he decided as he slotted bread into the toaster for his breakfast.

Once he'd eaten, he intended to go for a run and after that he'd do a few dozen laps of the local swimming pool. After that, maybe a little weight training would jolt his mind back into the sensible lane. If that didn't work either he would think of something else, although it was doubtful if he'd be fit to undertake any more exercise. He hadn't been lying when he'd told Eve that he had let his training lapse of late…

Eve.

Eve.

Red-gold hair.

Grey-green eyes.

Luscious curves.

Ryan cursed roundly as he exited the kitchen. Forget breakfast; he was going running now. And somewhere along the way he was going to outrun these thoughts that plagued him.

He followed the same route he had taken that night too, working on the principle that lightning didn't strike twice. It didn't either because he had rounded the bend when he spotted Eve coming towards him.

He slowed down, hurriedly debating his options. Should he turn around and head back the way he'd come or would that be too revealing? If he'd spotted Eve, she was bound to have seen him and he didn't want her to think that he had a problem with her even if he did.

One stride, two, and that was it; the decision was out of his hands. Ryan came to a halt, breathing far more heavily than the effort he'd expended warranted. It was just that seeing Eve made him feel breathless and giddy and all sorts of things he didn't normally feel. He groaned under his breath. Hell and damnation. He had a really big problem, Houston!

Eve came to a halt, her heart beating in rapid little jerks. She could lie to herself but what was the point? She had chosen to walk by the river because she had thought…hoped…that she might see Ryan here. That was the truth, although it wasn't all of it. She wasn't ready to work out why she'd wanted to see him when she had decided to keep well away from him. She would start with the easy bit and work up to the difficult bits later… Possibly.

'We meet again.' She gave a little laugh, wincing when she realised that it sounded like a rusty nail being scraped down a blackboard. Ryan was jogging on the spot, obviously keen to keep up the momentum, and she felt a spurt of irritation strike her. He could at least *pretend* to be pleased to see her, couldn't he?

'Looks like it.' He grinned at her, his handsome face breaking into the same wonderfully warm smile he'd treated her to the other night, and Eve was instantly mollified and smiled back.

'You're obviously a glutton for punishment.'

'Or desperate.' He laughed, a soft rumble emerging from his powerful chest. 'Can you imagine how mortifying it will be if I have to drop out after I've persuaded everyone else to take part in this challenge?'

He rolled his eyes and Eve laughed more naturally this time. 'It wouldn't look very good.'

'Too right it wouldn't.' He chuckled. 'Marie, for one, would never let me live it down,' he said, referring Marie Thomas, the paediatric unit's redoubtable ward sister.

Eve's brows rose. 'Is Marie taking part?'

'Yep. She's raised almost three hundred pounds in sponsorship pledges too.'

'That's fabulous!' she exclaimed, genuinely impressed.

'It is. We're on course to raise almost ten thousand pounds all told, which is a lot of money.'

'It certainly is. You'll have to put me down as a sponsor. Will fifty pounds be enough? I've no idea what the going rate is.'

'That would be brilliant. Thank you.'

He touched her hand in a spontaneous gesture of thanks and Eve did her best not to react, but it was like trying to turn back the tide. A rush of panic engulfed her and she gasped. Ryan bent and looked into her face, looked deep into her eyes, into her soul even, and she could see the anger burning inside him.

'I don't know who's responsible for the way you've changed, Eve, but whoever it was, he did a real number on you. I don't know if there's anything I can do but if there is, you only have to ask.' He stepped back and his face was set. 'I want to help you, Eve. If you'll let me.'

CHAPTER THREE

WHAT WAS SHE doing here?

Eve's head spun as she stared around the kitchen. There was so much colour in the room that her eyes were dazzled. Deep yellow walls, bright blue cupboards, multicoloured china stacked on the shelves. The kettle was red, the toaster purple, the washing-up bowl an eye-watering green. It was like finding herself slap-bang in the middle of a rainbow and she felt disorientated, confused. Her life was all shades of grey, from washed-out silver to deep, dark charcoal. Colour was something she couldn't handle. Colour hinted at extremes, at passion, at desire, at all the things she didn't want to experience.

Colour scared her too because it reflected her feelings for Ryan. She couldn't see him in terms of black and white or even charcoal and silver. He was imprinted in her head in glorious Technicolor exactly like this room.

'Sorry about that. It was my mother. She seems to have a knack of phoning when it's least convenient.'

Ryan came back into the room and Eve forced herself to concentrate. He'd put on a track suit over his running clothes, plain black, unadorned and mercifully lacking in colour. She watched as he headed to the gleaming red kettle and flicked the switch. She could hear the water hissing as it came to the boil, hear it getting louder and louder, and her senses were assaulted once more, only by noise this time. If she didn't *do* colour then she didn't do noise either!

She shot to her feet, almost overturning the chair in her haste to escape. Ryan glanced round, his expression as bland as a baby's. She knew he could tell how panicstricken she felt but he didn't ask her what was wrong or offer suggestions to calm her down. He simply accepted her turmoil and for some reason she felt better because of it.

'At least have a cup of coffee before you go. It'll only take a couple of seconds to make it.'

He took a pair of mugs off a shelf and spooned instant coffee granules into them then topped them up with boiling water. The milk was in the fridge—the jug was orange—the sugar in a bowl that had multicoloured spots on it. He dumped everything on the table and sat down, leaving her to decide what she intended to do.

She could go or she could stay and it was all the same to him, he was trying to imply, only she knew it wasn't how he really felt. Not inside. Ryan wanted her to stay. And he wanted her to stay because he cared. That was why he had insisted she should come home with him, but did she want him to care? That was the big question, the one she couldn't answer now and maybe not ever.

'Fancy a biscuit? Or how about some toast?'

He half rose but Eve shook her head and he subsided back onto his chair. Picking up his mug, he drank a little coffee, blowing on the glassy black surface first to cool it. Eve averted her eyes, not wanting to watch how his lips puckered as he sucked in air then blew it out in a soft little sigh that seemed ridiculously loud to her hypersensitive ears. She didn't want her senses to stir from their slumbers again, didn't want to feel attraction or anything else. She just wanted to *be,* with all that did and didn't entail.

Silence fell as she sat down and unconsciously she started counting the minutes. How long would it last, this silence? One minute? Ten? She'd come to dread the silences when she'd been with Damien. When he wasn't talking, he was thinking and she had learned to fear his thoughts as much as his actions. Damien could turn peace and quiet into terror in the blink of an eye so she had chattered on, inane comments aimed at soothing him, even though they had rarely worked.

Tears started to her eyes as the memories came flooding back and she stared into her coffee, wishing she could sink into its dark heart and disappear. She couldn't do this. She wasn't brave enough to gather up the threads and learn how to be herself again.

'Tell me, Eve. I can't promise it will help but it might and that has to be better than this.'

Ryan's voice was so calm, so patient, so free of threat that Eve felt a little of the fear trickle out of her. She shrugged, her hands cradling the mug because it was something to hold onto.

'What's to tell? I think you've guessed already, haven't you?'

'Guessing is one thing. Hearing about what you've been through is something else.'

He half reached towards her then stopped and pain rippled under her skin. He wouldn't touch her again. He knew how she felt about being touched because she had made it clear. Maybe she should be relieved yet it was more proof of how much she had changed. Ryan had often put his arm around her in the past, often hugged her in a friendly fashion, and all of a sudden she missed being on the receiving end of his warmth and kindness, missed being normal. If she could learn to give and receive the odd hug, it would mean she was on her way to finding the person she had been.

'I was in an abusive relationship. It took me almost two years to pluck up the courage to leave and I'm still getting over what happened.'

'You did well to get out when you did. A lot of women never find the strength to cut the ties.'

His tone was level. There was no hint of censure for her or for her abuser but Eve wasn't fooled. Ryan hated the thought of her being treated so badly and a little more fear trickled away and a tiny bit of warmth took its place.

'I didn't think I'd have the strength either, which is funny, really, because I always thought that I would never put up with being abused. We used to see women like that when we were doing our rotations, didn't we?' She carried on when he nodded, suddenly eager to explain why she had allowed it to happen to her. 'I could never understand why they let their husbands or boyfriends treat them the way they did, but it's different when it happens to you.'

'I remember one woman telling me that she hated what was happening and hated herself even more for allowing it to happen, but she didn't know how to stop it.'

His voice was still calm, uncritical, relaxed. They could have been discussing the price of fish for all the emotion he betrayed but Eve knew it was an act. Ryan cared. He really cared. She clung to that thought. 'She loved her partner and couldn't imagine a life without him, I expect.'

'It's all part of it, isn't it?' He shrugged. 'The abuser makes his victim so dependent on him that she finds it impossible to imagine not being with him.'

'Or her. There are men who are victims of abuse too.'

'True, although not as many men suffer abuse as women do.'

'No.' Eve swallowed, feeling sick. It always happened whenever she had to admit that she was a victim of abuse. Oh, she might know that she was, but knowing it and admitting it were two very different things.

'How did it start?' Ryan prompted, and she forced the nausea down. Now that she had got this far, she wanted to carry on to the end, surprisingly enough.

'Exactly as you read about it in all the textbooks.' She gave a little laugh and he laughed too and it made her feel better, as though they were in this together. It was such a crazy idea that she immediately dismissed it. Ryan wasn't part of this and he never would be. She was the one who had to learn to cope, to live, to forgive herself.

'Damien was so charming, so funny, so sexy, and

I was completely smitten. I never realised how controlling he was until it was too late.' She shrugged. 'I found it touching that he wanted to see me every night, that he hated me going out with friends, that he loathed us being apart. I thought it showed his vulnerable side and that's something a lot of women find attractive. I certainly did.'

'So when did you realise that it wasn't vulnerability that was making him behave that way?'

Ryan's voice sounded deeper and she shivered. Was her story getting to him? Was he really thinking how stupid she'd been to be taken in? She tried not to let the idea take hold but it was hard when it was what she herself believed.

'It was a gradual process. Damien started to object whenever I said I was going out so, to keep the peace, I stopped making arrangements to see my friends. Then, because I always refused to go out with them, they stopped asking me.'

'So he got what he wanted? He isolated you. Classic behaviour, as you said.'

'Exactly.' She managed a little smile. 'I should write a paper on this, shouldn't I? Only I doubt it would make any difference. Far too many women are as gullible as me.'

'It's not gullible to believe that someone loves you. It's what everyone wants, to love and be loved.'

'Is that what you want?' she asked before she could think better of it.

'Probably.'

'But you never went out with anyone for more than

a couple of months, did you? You had quite a reputation for playing the field.'

'Did I?' He shrugged but she knew that he had taken her comment to heart and wished she hadn't said anything. She had enough to do with sorting out her own life without trying to find out what made Ryan tick.

The thought that there was something behind his behaviour was intriguing. She had to make a determined effort to dismiss it. 'Anyway, once Damien had control of my social life, he set about controlling my working life too.'

Eve stopped and took a deep breath as the full impact of that statement assailed her. Losing her friends had been bad enough, but losing her career had been so much worse. She had thrown everything away, given in to the threats and the coercion because she'd been afraid of upsetting Damien. All those years of study, of hard work and determination had been reduced to nothing because she had been a coward.

'In what way did he take over your working life?'

Ryan's voice grated and Eve steered her thoughts away from herself. Although she wanted him to know the truth, she didn't want it to have a detrimental effect on him too. It was enough that her life had been blighted by her stupidity.

'Oh, it was pure textbook stuff once again,' she said with an insouciance she didn't feel. 'You know, the odd comment that made me doubt my judgement or a look that implied I was mistaken. Damien often conducted ward rounds, if you remember. The consultant was rarely there so there were dozens of opportunities when he could belittle me. And he made the most of them, believe me.'

'I never realised.' Ryan frowned. 'I can remember him being rather sharp with you a few times but I thought he was trying to make it appear that he didn't favour you. Everyone knew you two were an item and I assumed he didn't want anyone complaining that you had an unfair advantage.'

'No chance of that.' She smiled bitterly. 'I was never going to get a boost up the career ladder if Damien had anything to do with it.'

'It must have been a nightmare for you, Eve. Did you never think of telling anyone?'

'No. By the time I realised what was happening, it was too late. I was too ashamed of letting myself be sucked in and too afraid of Damien to speak out.'

Ryan stared at his coffee. He was gripping the mug so hard that the bones in his hands gleamed white through his skin. He forced himself to relax his grip, afraid that he would crush the china, not that it mattered. What did a broken cup matter? Eve had been put through the wringer and spat out the other side and he'd been so intent on making sure that *he* didn't get involved that he'd allowed it to happen. Even though he'd had no idea what had been going on, he would never get over the guilt he felt for letting her down.

'I'm sorry, Eve. I know it's too late, but I'm really and truly sorry I wasn't there for you.' He looked up, met her eyes, and felt worse than ever. She had needed him and he had failed her; what sort of a person did that make him?

'You weren't to know, Ryan. I made sure you didn't

know, in fact.' She gave a hoarse little laugh. 'I became extremely adept at concealing the evidence.'

'You mean the bruises?' Ryan heard the disgust in his voice, not at what she had done by hiding the evidence but at what had been done to her, although he realised too late that it was what she thought.

'Yes, although Damien was careful not to hit me where it showed most of the time.'

Ryan couldn't bear it. He simply couldn't bear to hear her sounding so apologetic. *She* was the victim. And *she* was the one who should be reaping all the apologies.

'Obviously a man of many talents,' he said roughly, pushing back his chair. He went over to the kettle, although he doubted if he could drink any more coffee without it choking him. Still, he had to do something, had to take the edge off the moment and make it more bearable for her.

She had been so brave to tell him what she had. He had dealt with other victims of abuse and he knew how hard they found it to speak about their experiences. There was all the shame as well as the misplaced guilt, the thought that somehow they had brought it upon themselves. He couldn't bear to think that Eve believed she was responsible for what had happened to her, although he wouldn't be surprised if she did.

He swung round. 'What happened wasn't your fault, Eve. You do understand that?'

'Yes and no.' She shrugged, avoiding his eyes as she stared at point above his left shoulder. 'Intellectually I understand it but emotionally...well, it's a different story.'

Ryan swore under his breath as he sat down. He leant across the table, his frustration rising because he didn't dare touch her. Would they ever reach a point where he could? he wondered. A point where she wouldn't shrink away and would welcome his touch? He had no idea yet all of a sudden it seemed incredibly important that it should happen. He *needed* to touch Eve, for his sake as well as for hers. She may have been absent from his life for several years but he wanted her to be part of it from now on.

The thought barely had a chance to filter through the receptors in his brain when there was a loud hammering on the cottage door. Ryan stood up, frowning as he glanced along the hall.

'I wonder who that is,' he said, his voice sounding rough thanks to all the emotions he'd had to contend with in the past half hour. He had slipped into a comfortable routine over the years. Although he dated frequently, he never gave one hundred per cent of himself to a relationship. There was always a couple of per cent held in reserve, a bit of himself going spare.

It was safer that way. If he held something back, he could remain focused on his objectives, i.e. keeping Scott's name alive and raising money to prevent other families going through what his family had gone through. However, he knew that if he involved himself in Eve's affairs, he wouldn't be able to do that. He would have to give her one hundred per cent of himself and he wasn't sure if it would be wise. Something warned him that every little bit he gave to Eve would make him want to give even more and where would that leave him? In over his head, in so deep that he'd never surface?

He had avoided love and avoided it for one very important reason: he didn't want to be responsible for ruining some woman's life. What if he fell in love, got married, had a child and, like Scott, it died? Although he wasn't affected by the genetic abnormality that had caused his brother's death, he could pass it on to his own children. That was why he was never going to have children and why he was never going to marry either. It wouldn't be fair to enter into marriage on that basis. Maybe the woman would accept it at first, but what if she changed her mind? What if she decided that she wanted a family and he refused? How could any marriage survive that kind of pressure?

As he made his way to the door, Ryan realised that no matter how he felt about Eve, it wasn't enough. Was that why he had stuck to friendship in the past? Why he had deliberately distanced himself after that kiss? Had he known, subconsciously, that Eve was the woman who could make him reconsider his decision to remain single?

With a sudden rush of insight, he knew it was true and it made him even more determined not to get involved with her on anything more than a friendly basis. Eve had been through enough, without him ruining her life as well.

Ryan's heart was heavy as he opened the door. He frowned when he found his neighbour, Maureen Roberts, on the step. She was soaking wet, dripping water and river slime all over the doormat.

'We need your help, Ryan,' she said before he

could speak. 'A boy's fallen into the river and he's not breathing. My Frank pulled him out but he's not sure what to do.'

'Right. Have you phoned for an ambulance?' Ryan asked immediately.

'No. Frank's phone won't work. It was in his trouser pocket when he jumped into the water.'

'No problem.' Ryan glanced round when he heard footsteps and felt his heart lift when he saw Eve before he ruthlessly brought it back down to earth. No ringing bells, no shooting stars—just friendship.

'Can you phone for an ambulance? A boy's fallen into the river and he isn't breathing. I'm going to see what I can do to help.'

He turned and jogged down the path, not waiting to see if Eve did as he'd asked. He knew she would, knew too that she would follow and help him. They were certainties like the sun rising each morning and setting each night and he could cope with them. What he couldn't handle were all the unanswered questions buzzing around inside his head. Could he stick to being Eve's friend? Or would he end up wanting more than friendship? And if he did, could he resist? Or would he give in?

He ran down the path to the river, ran as though his life depended on him getting there, but no matter how fast he went, he couldn't outrun the questions.

Did he?

Would he?

Should he?

Could he?

He wished he knew!

CHAPTER FOUR

THEY CARRIED ON trying to resuscitate the boy long after it became clear that it was hopeless. Eve took over again, pumping the child's thin chest while Ryan breathed into his mouth. She wanted to tell him to stop, wanted to assure him that they'd done everything possible, but she couldn't seem to find the words. How could she tell him that life was extinct when it was obviously so important to him that they save the boy?

The ambulance arrived at last and it was a relief to let the paramedics take over. Ryan supervised as the crew followed procedure and gave the boy a shot of adrenaline then tried to defibrillate him. They tried twice more but the result was the same: a flat, unwavering line on the screen. The boy was gone and now all that could be done for him was to inform his parents.

Ryan's face was set as they watched the ambulance quietly drive away. There was no need for flashing lights or sirens now, Eve thought sadly. She forced herself to smile when Maureen came over to them, seeking reassurance.

'We did everything possible, Maureen. There's no knowing how long he'd been in the water before your husband saw him, so the odds were against us from the outset.'

'I know that, love. It's just so hard when it's a child, isn't it?' Maureen's face crumpled and tears rolled down her cheeks. 'Those poor parents. I can't imagine how awful it's going to be for them when they find out.'

'I know,' Eve agreed sadly. 'Is he a local child, do you know?'

'No. Apparently, the family's here on holiday. They've rented a caravan over at Fulbrook Farm,' Maureen explained, sniffing noisily. Her husband appeared just then, grey-faced with shock, and led her away.

Eve sighed as she turned to Ryan, who had been standing silently to one side. 'That's it, then. There's nothing more we can do.'

She thought he hadn't heard her at first but then he nodded. Swinging round on his heel, he led the way up the path, pausing briefly to give the police officer who had attended the scene his name and address. Eve gave hers as well, nodding when she was informed that she would be required to make a statement later. It was procedure and she would do what had to be done even though it gave her no pleasure. A young life had been lost and it was a tragedy.

Was that why it had had such an impact on Ryan? Had it reminded him of losing his brother? He had never told her how his twin had died but it could explain why he seemed so deeply affected by what happened. Eve bit her lip as she followed him into the house. Whilst she didn't want to become too involved in his affairs, she couldn't walk away when he needed her. It wouldn't be fair, especially after the way he had listened to her, listened and not judged her as he'd had every right to do. He had been a good friend in the past and he had been a good friend today too. Talking to him had made her feel so much better.

The thought surprised her, although she didn't dwell on it. Walking over to the kettle, she switched it on and then turned to him. 'I could do with a drink. How about you?'

He shrugged. 'Fine.'

He sat down, his face shuttered, his eyes blank, and Eve knew she was right. This had as much to do with losing his brother as it had with them failing to save the boy's life. Pulling out a chair, she sat down, feeling a little flutter of alarm in the centre of her chest. If she asked him to tell her about his brother, it would be even harder to keep her distance, but how could she not ask? Not try to help? It would be a mark of cowardice and she refused to be a coward ever again.

'I hope I'm not speaking out of turn but I can see that this has affected you. Has it brought back memories of your brother?'

'How did you guess?' He sighed as he tipped back his chair and stared at the ceiling. Eve had a feeling that he didn't want her to see just how much it had affected him and felt hurt before she realised how silly it was. Her feelings didn't matter; it was how Ryan felt that was important.

'What happened to him?' she asked, trying to inject a degree of objectivity into her voice that she didn't feel. She *cared* that Ryan was hurting and it worried her. She was too emotionally scarred to find the right balance and it would be far too easy to get swept along in a direction she shouldn't take.

'He suffered a cardiac arrest. There was no warning. He just dropped down onto the ground and died.'

'How awful!' she exclaimed. 'It must have been a terrible shock for you and your parents.'

'It was.' His tone was flat. Eve guessed that it was the only way he could talk about what had happened, by keeping his emotions under control. 'Scott was always superbly fit. He was a brilliant footballer—he played centre forward for our school—and he took his training really seriously. He wanted to turn professional and he would have made it too. He was actually playing a match when he died. There was a scout there for one of the big league clubs and Scott was just superb, and then all of a sudden he fell to the ground.'

He stopped, his expression so bleak that Eve's heart ached for him. Reaching out, she touched his hand, unaware of what she was doing. She just wanted to comfort him, to console him, to offer anything she could that might help to ease his pain.

'I'm so sorry, Ryan. Really I am.'

'Thank you.' He dredged up a smile. 'It's got easier with time but it still upsets me whenever I think about it.'

'It's bound to.' She withdrew her hand, suddenly realising what she had done. A shiver passed through her, although for some reason she didn't feel as panic-stricken as she might have expected. She cleared her throat, not wanting to explore that idea either. 'Do you know what actually happened to him?'

'Yes. It was long QT syndrome.'

'That's a disorder of the heart's electrical system, isn't it?' Eve clarified.

'That's right. The QT interval is a measurement on the ECG tracing that reflects the electrical activity in the ventricles. In LQTS the length of time it takes the electrical system to recharge itself after each heartbeat is longer than normal. This can create a very rapid, irregular heart rhythm, which results in no blood being pumped from the heart. If that happens the brain is deprived of oxygen, causing a sudden loss of consciousness or even death.' He grimaced. 'Sorry. You must know all that. I'm just so used to explaining it at various fundraising events that it's second nature to trot out the whole spiel.'

'It's fine,' she assured him. 'Anyway, it's good to be reminded of the details. I have to admit that I've never dealt with a case of LQTS. It's quite rare, isn't it?'

'Not as rare as you think. It causes between three and four thousand deaths in children and young adults in the United States alone.'

'Really?' Eve couldn't hide her surprise. 'I had no idea.'

'I was surprised too. LQTS affects about one person in ten thousand, so it was a shock to discover how many people die as a result of it.'

'Nobody knew that your brother had it?'

'No. As I said, Scott was superbly fit. He played a lot of other sports as well as football and was always very active. It was a real bolt from the blue.'

'It must have been.' Eve hesitated. Every question she asked would mean that she was that bit more involved and yet she knew that she wanted to know as much as possible if it meant she could help him. 'It can be hereditary, can't it?'

'Yes. Once it was established why Scott had died, we were all tested. A couple of cousins had also died when they were teenagers—one drowned while swimming and another died in his sleep. Taken singly they appeared to be terrible tragedies but they also pointed towards there being a genetic abnormality in the family. Sadly, it turned out to be true.'

'I see. So are you all right? You said that you and Scott were twins…' She tailed off, wondering why she felt so fearful at the thought of Ryan suffering the same tragic end as his brother. She took a deep breath and made herself calm down. It wouldn't help if she let him see how alarmed she felt.

'I'm fine. I'm not affected by the faulty gene, although a couple of cousins are. They've been put on beta blockers and they're fine, I'm happy to say.'

'Good job they were tested.' Eve sighed. 'It's just a shame that your brother never showed any sign of illness beforehand.'

'It is.' He summoned a smile, although his eyes were bleak. 'Still, these things happen, don't they?'

'They do, although that doesn't make it any less painful, especially after what happened today.' She touched his hand again, felt a tiny frisson ripple under her skin, and quickly withdrew. Maybe it wasn't fear that had prompted it but she wasn't sure if it was equally dangerous to feel pleasure either.

'It just got to me, I'm afraid. Normally, I'm able to

take a more balanced view but I was already feeling emotional and I don't think that helped.'

'Because of what I'd told you?' she said quietly.

'Yes.'

He didn't prevaricate but simply told the truth and Eve was grateful for that. She would hate him to think that he had to lie to spare her feelings. Honesty was something that had been in short supply during her time with Damien. She had lied to her friends, lied to her parents and lied to her colleagues too. That Damien had told even more lies than her was another factor. It made her value Ryan's honesty all the more.

'I'm sorry, Ryan. I never meant to upset you.'

'I know you didn't. And no matter how much it upset me to hear what you've been through, I wouldn't have it any other way.'

He looked into her eyes and she shivered when she saw the expression his held. There was so much tenderness, so much concern, so much...*everything* that her heart began to race. It had been ages since anyone had looked at her this way. Looked at her as though she was precious, special; looked at her not because they wanted something from her but because they wanted to *do* something for her. It made her feel different inside, less alone, less isolated, and it was a strange feeling after the years she'd spent mentally and physically segregated from the world.

'It helped to tell you,' she admitted, needing to repay his honesty with the truth. 'I feel less alone, I suppose.'

'I'm glad.'

He smiled at her, his face lighting up in the way

that she'd always found so attractive in the past. That she found it very attractive these days too was clear and the thought alarmed her. Pushing back her chair, she stood up.

'Right. I'd better go. I've a load of jobs that need doing.'

She hurried to the door, hearing the scrape of chair legs as Ryan got up as well. She'd told him more than she had told anyone else and whilst it was true that it had helped, she found herself wondering if she had gone too far. It would be that much harder to maintain her distance now, to keep him at arm's length where he had to remain. The fact was that she had nothing to offer him. Nothing worth sharing.

'If you need me, Eve, you know where I am.'

Ryan stopped by the bottom of the stairs as she opened the front door. Did he understand how she felt? Eve wondered, glancing back. Understand that she was afraid of getting involved? She sensed it was true and for some reason it made her feel better. Ryan wouldn't push her into doing anything she didn't want to do.

'Thank you.' She smiled at him. 'I appreciate that, Ryan, more than you can imagine.'

He gave a brief nod but didn't say anything else as she stepped out of the door. She hurried down the path, crossing the road so she could take the same route home that they had taken to get there. She was still finding her way around the town and she didn't want to get lost, although she could always phone Ryan and ask him to come and rescue her if that happened.

Eve sighed. She mustn't start to see Ryan as her knight in shining armour—it wouldn't be fair. She could end up as a liability to him and that was something she refused to be. Ryan shouldn't have to pick up the pieces and put her back together. She had to do that herself.

If she could.

Ryan went to the police station on Sunday morning and gave a statement. He half expected to see Eve there and was relieved when there was no sign of her. Once the formalities were completed, he went home and changed into his running clothes, taking a different route this time rather than run the risk of bumping into her again.

He sighed as he toiled up the hill. He couldn't keep avoiding her, especially when they worked together. However, he needed breathing space, time to get his emotions in hand. What she had told him had had a big effect and he needed to put everything into perspective. If he didn't do so, he would become even more involved and that was something he couldn't afford. He had nothing to offer Eve, nothing to offer *any* woman. He had to remember that and not be seduced by all these unfamiliar emotions running riot inside him.

Monday rolled around and it was a relief to go into work. At least while he was working he would be able to forget about Eve, he reasoned as he made his way to Paediatrics. He sighed as he pushed open the office door and saw her sitting behind the desk.

Who was he kidding? He couldn't forget about Eve in or out of work!

'You're early. Getting a head start, are you?'

'Something like that.'

She looked up and smiled but Ryan saw the wariness in her eyes and realised that she'd been having as tough a time as him. Eve was finding it equally hard to put *him* out of *her* mind and the thought was the last thing he needed. How in heaven's name was he going to keep his distance when he knew she was struggling as well?

'Anything I need to know?' he asked, trying his best to get his thoughts back on track and keep them there.

'We had an admission in the early hours of the morning that you need to take a look at.' She turned her attention to the monitor and Ryan knew—he just knew!—that she, too, was redirecting her thoughts along a safer route.

'Ten-year-old boy called George Porter. He's been complaining of headaches for the past few days. He also had a temperature so Mum thought he probably had a bug and has been dosing him with paracetamol to keep his temperature down. Last night he seemed much worse, though, and she brought him into A and E.'

'What did they say?' Ryan queried.

'They decided it was some sort of viral infection and told the mother to carry on with what she'd been doing and sent him home.' She sighed. 'Anyway, he woke up in the early hours, screaming, and told his mum that his head was bursting, so she called an ambulance.'

'I see. We'd better take a look at him, then.'

Ryan led the way into the ward, waiting for Eve to point him in the right direction. George was in the end bay and he was obviously a very sick little boy. His mother was with him and Ryan smiled at her as he introduced himself. 'Hello, Mrs Porter. I'm Ryan Sullivan, the senior registrar. Dr Pascoe has filled me in on what's happened so let's see if we can get George sorted out, shall we?'

'I hope so, Dr Sullivan,' Andrea Porter replied anxiously.

Ryan bent over the child, taking his time as he examined him. With symptoms like these, there could be any number of things causing the problem. He checked the boy's reaction to light, which was normal, then felt around the base of his neck, frowning when he discovered a definite rigidity in the muscles. 'Feel his neck,' he said quietly, glancing at Eve.

He moved aside so she could take his place, sucking in his breath when her arm brushed his as she bent over the bed. He could feel his skin tingling, tiny ripples of sensation, light as snowflakes, dancing across its surface. It was an effort not to show how alarmed he felt as he waited for her to finish because he didn't *do* this sort of thing, didn't react this way when a woman touched him. It made him see just how deep he was in and he bit back a groan.

Maybe he didn't want to get too involved but he might not have a choice!

CHAPTER FIVE

'THERE'S A DEFINITE stiffness about the neck.'

Eve smoothed her face into what she hoped was a noncommittal expression before she looked up. She could feel flurries of sensation rippling through her body and fought to ignore them. So what if she had touched Ryan? It had been an accident, unlike yesterday when she had deliberately laid her hand on his arm in an attempt to comfort him.

The thought wasn't the best she could have come up with, certainly not the ideal one to calm her down, so it was a relief to discover that Ryan wasn't looking at her. He bent over the child again, rolling up George's pyjama legs and frowning when he saw the blotchy red rash on the boy's shins.

'When did this rash appear?' he demanded, glancing at Eve.

'I've no idea. It definitely wasn't there when I examined him earlier,' she explained. 'Is it what I think it might be?'

'Yes. It looks very much like the rash you'd expect to see in cases of meningococcal meningitis.' He ignored Mrs Porter's horrified gasp as he reached for a drinking glass off the bedside locker. Pressing it against the rash, he nodded. 'See. The rash doesn't disappear when I press this glass against it. It's meningitis all right and we need to get it sorted out a.s.a.p.'

He pushed back the curtain and left, leaving Eve to console George's mother. The poor woman was shaking uncontrollably and Eve honestly thought she was going to pass out. She filled a second glass with water and handed it toher.

'Take a sip of this and if you still feel faint, put your head between your knees.'

Mrs Porter did as she was told and gradually her colour returned. 'Do you think it's meningitis?' she asked anxiously.

'It looks very much like it,' Eve told her gently.

'But why didn't they realise what it was last night when I took George into A and E?'

'I don't know.' Eve shrugged, although she couldn't help thinking that whoever had examined the child had been very remiss for not considering the possibility. 'Sometimes it's difficult to make an accurate diagnosis until all the symptoms have appeared.'

'I suppose so,' Mrs Porter conceded. She looked up when Ryan reappeared. He had Marie Thomas, the ward sister, with him and they wasted no time setting up a drip.

'I'm going to give George intravenous antibiotics,' he explained, swiftly inserting a cannula into the boy's arm. He waited while Marie linked up the line then started the drip running. 'We need to get them into him as quickly as possible. That way he'll have the best chance.'

Mrs Porter shuddered. 'It's bad, isn't it, Doctor?'

'I'm afraid so. Obviously, we need to take a sample of cerebrospinal fluid to confirm the diagnosis but I'm fairly certain that's what it is.' He sighed. 'I only wish we'd realised what we were dealing with sooner than this.'

'It's not your fault,' the mother countered. 'If anyone's to blame, it's that doctor I saw in A and E. I wasn't impressed by his attitude at the time, to be frank. He couldn't have cared less about George—he was more concerned about answering his mobile phone. Just wait till my husband finds out. He won't let this lie, you mark my words.'

'It's often difficult to make an accurate diagnosis when there's so little to go on,' Ryan pointed out, unwittingly repeating what Eve had said.

She shivered, wondering why it made her feel both elated and scared to know they were in accord. It had happened in the past, too, she recalled. They had worked together during their rotations and more often than not they had reached the same conclusions. They'd used to laugh about it, in fact, teased each other about reading one another's minds.

They'd been such happy days, she thought sadly. What a fool she had been to give them up for the sake of love, or what she had believed to be love. Now she knew better. She had been dazzled by Damien's charm, seduced by his flattery.

She'd been so hurt when Ryan had distanced himself after the Christmas party. She had honestly thought they'd had something special when he had kissed her so her confidence had been rocked when she'd realised that he didn't think that. To have someone as sophisticated and worldly as Damien pay her attention had been a sop to her pride. Had Damien realised how vulnerable she'd been and was that why he had chosen her? Because she'd been malleable, gullible, a potential victim?

It was upsetting to wonder if she had given that impression. It reinforced her decision not to get involved again. If it could happen once it could happen a second time, although she need have no worries on that score when it came to Ryan. He would never treat her that way. Never in a million years.

The thought was unsettling because it was yet another positive thought about Ryan. If she weren't careful, she would find herself getting too attached to him and that would never do. Eve tried not to dwell on it as she filled in George's chart. He would need to be moved from the main ward so once his file was updated, she went and made arrangements to have him moved to PHDU.

Ryan stayed behind to explain to his mother what needed to be done to collect the necessary samples. Eve knew how distressing it could be for a parent to hear that a needle would be inserted into their child's spinal cord but if anyone could make it easier, it was Ryan. He had the gift of making people trust him and it was another thought that caused her more than a little unease. That she too was willing to trust him was a given, even though she should be as wary of him as any other man. But Ryan was different—she viewed him differently. There was no escaping that fact no matter how hard she tried.

* * *

The day flew past, every minute filled with work, and Ryan was glad. He always enjoyed being busy and he enjoyed it even more that day. At least while he was working he couldn't keep thinking about Eve, although heaven knew what would happen when he went home. He sighed as he punched the button for the lift. He still hadn't got over what had gone on earlier. Eve had touched him and he still bore the effects of it. Why, he only had to recall the light pressure of her arm on his and he went weak at the knees!

Marie was waiting when he got back to the unit. 'So, what's the story from A and E?'

'I've not got to the bottom of it yet.' Ryan shrugged. Out of the corner of his eye he saw Eve walking down the ward and turned so he could avoid looking at her. There was no point testing himself again. 'I had a word with Harry Summers, the senior reg, and apparently it was an agency doctor who dealt with George. Harry's going to try and find out what went on, but he's not hopeful that he'll come up with any answers as to why the boy was sent home without any tests being done.'

'Typical!' Marie snorted. 'They hire agency staff rather than employ full-time staff to save money and then wonder why it all goes wrong.'

'There's no saying it did go wrong,' Ryan pointed out, wanting to be fair. He heard footsteps behind him and stiffened because he knew they belonged to Eve. He didn't need to check, he just knew, and it was another indication of how deep he was in. Some-how he had to keep one foot on solid ground otherwise he would fall hook, line and sinker into Eve's life and affairs.

'I suppose so,' Marie conceded, grudgingly. 'Anyway, there's no point us worrying about it, is there? You still on for tonight?'

'Tonight?' Ryan repeated, because his brain seemed to have stalled on that thought. He breathed in, hoping the extra oxygen would kick-start it into working again, and realised immediately what a mistake that was. Along with the oxygen came something far more dangerous, something that made his heart race and his senses reel, something that could only be Eve's perfume. He groaned as he inhaled the delicate floral fragrance. Forget having one foot on solid ground. He was already in free-fall!

'It's curry night, of course! Don't tell me you've forgotten? You must be losing it if you don't remember important social events like this!'

Marie laughed and Ryan joined in, although it was an effort in view of the thoughts that were rioting around his head. He couldn't afford to let his emotions get the better of him. He had to remember all the reasons why it would be wrong to get involved with Eve. However, it was proving harder than it should have been.

'Probably my age,' he retorted drolly, determined to take control of himself. 'I'm reaching a point where I have difficulty remembering things.'

'Then pity help you when you get to my age is all I can say,' Marie said pithily. 'Anyway, to refresh your failing memory, we're meeting at seven o'clock at Taste of India. OK?'

'Fine.' Ryan glanced round when Eve went to walk past them. He had no idea why he said what he did next. He certainly hadn't planned on saying it when he should be keeping his distance and yet all of a sudden the words flowed from his lips. 'How about it, Eve? You used to love a good curry so why don't you come along?'

Eve put down the lipstick and studied herself in the mirror. She'd made a real effort tonight and she had to admit that she was pleased with the result. After washing and drying her hair, she'd left it to fall around her shoulders in loose red-gold waves, rather than pinning it back into the severe style she favoured these days. Although she never used much make-up, muted green eyeshadow and a layer of mascara made her eyes look huge and luminous. Soft peach lip gloss emphasised the fullness of her lips and toned with the peach sweater she had decided to wear.

She looked good and she knew it but was it a mistake to take so much trouble over her appearance? Was it a mistake to go, in fact? Surely it would make her life more complicated if she started socialising with the rest of the staff. At the moment nobody knew about her past, apart from Ryan, but once she got to know everyone better they would be bound to ask questions. How could she explain why she had taken four years off from her studies without telling them about Damien?

Panic gripped her and she gasped. She breathed deeply, in and out, as she'd been taught to do, and after a moment it passed. Picking up her bag, she headed to the door. Damien had been out of her life for years now and she resented the fact that he could still influence her behaviour in any way. She had to go to tonight if only to prove to herself that she would be free of him one day.

It was a warm evening so she decided to walk into town. She was almost there when she heard someone calling her name and looked round to see Ryan crossing the road. He grinned as he joined her on the pavement and Eve did her best to stop her heart leaping right out of her chest. However, he looked so handsome in a deep blue sweater that highlighted his dark good looks and she couldn't help being aware of it.

'You were walking so fast that I didn't think I was going to catch up with you. You must be starving 'cos you obviously can't wait to tuck into your curry!'

'How did you guess?' Eve laughed, doing her best to act naturally. It wasn't easy, though, when her heart seemed to be performing its very own gymnastic display. He looked both handsome and *fit*, and there was no denying that everything female inside her was responding to him.

'It's ages since I had a decent curry,' she said hurriedly, terrified that he would read her mind. Maybe Ryan was nothing like Damien and wouldn't try to use her feelings to his advantage but it was too soon to feel this way. She needed to find herself first, rediscover the person she was, and that was hard enough. She didn't need any added complications in her life that might stop her achieving that goal.

'Well, you won't find a better curry than they serve at Taste of India. It's one of our favourite haunts and

I'm only glad you decided to come along, Eve.' His smile was gentle, filled with understanding, and her heart managed another couple of somersaults.

'It was kind of you to invite me,' she said politely, although she could hear how breathless she sounded. That Ryan must have noticed it too was obvious but he didn't say anything as they started walking again and she couldn't help thinking how typical it was of him. Ryan would never put her on the spot, never try to make her feel uncomfortable, and it was such a relief to know that she didn't need to be on her guard.

Since she'd returned to medicine, she had put up a protective shield, wary of letting people know how vulnerable she was. However, there was no need to do that with Ryan. She could be honest with him and not have to hide. Eve realised that it was the first step towards reclaiming her life. Once she got used to being open with Ryan, it would be easier to behave that way with other people too.

That encouraging thought accompanied her as they made their way to the restaurant. Marie was already there, along with a couple of other nurses, and they greeted her with genuine enthusiasm. Eve felt herself relax that bit more and it was a wonderful feeling to be able to let go after all the tension that had filled her life. For the first time in ages she felt normal.

Ryan did his best, he really did, but he couldn't keep his eyes off Eve. She looked so different tonight, relaxed and happy, and he couldn't help wondering what had brought about the change in her. Was she finally getting over her experiences with Damien? He hoped so. Nobody should have to go through what she'd been through and he resolved right then and there that he would do everything in his power to help her. Eve needed him to be her friend more than ever now.

The thought struck a chord, one he wouldn't allow himself to dwell on. There was no point thinking that he would like to be more than a friend when it wasn't going to happen. He joined in the conversation, laughing as Marie recounted a tale about the parents who had mistakenly thought their child was going to have a *canal* put in her hand rather than a cannula. They had been deeply relieved when they had found out exactly what was going to happen.

'It's easy to forget that folk don't always understand the jargon,' he said when everyone stopped laughing. 'It's second nature to us but it must sound like double Dutch to a lot of people.'

'It might help if the parents were given a sort of glossary explaining the various procedures,' Eve suggested.

Ryan nodded. 'That's a good idea, actually. It would prevent a lot of confusion. I know we find it funny but it's hard enough for the parents without them having to struggle to work out what's happening to their child.'

'I could put something together if you like,' she offered.

'Would you?' Ryan grinned at her, loving the fact that she looked so animated. She looked like the old Eve, happy and full of enthusiasm, and it was good to know that she hadn't been completely destroyed by her ex's appalling treatment.

'I'd be very careful if I were you.' Marie shook an admonishing finger at them and for a moment Ryan wondered if the older woman had picked up on his thoughts. Had Marie sensed that he was attracted to Eve and was she keen to warn her not to expect too much from him? He knew that he had a reputation for playing the field, although he always took great care to ensure that nobody got hurt. However, the thought that Marie might feel it necessary to warn Eve off didn't sit well with him.

'I'm sure there's no need to worry,' he began, but Marie cut him off.

'*No need to worry*!' Marie snorted. 'I've seen that gleam in your eyes before, Ryan Sullivan, and in my experience it means only one thing: you've found yourself another poor sucker.' She turned to Eve and grinned. 'Before you know it, he'll have you doing all sorts of things you never bargained for. You mark my words, love. Ryan is a master at getting folk to do whatever he wants!'

Everyone laughed, Eve included, but Ryan heard the strain in her voice and winced. Whilst he hoped she had taken Marie's comments in the spirit in which they'd been meant, he couldn't be sure, especially after everything she had been through. The thought plagued him throughout the evening. He knew he wouldn't rest until he had spoken to Eve and made sure she understood that Marie had been joking. It was a relief when everyone started to make a move because it meant he would be able to clear up any misunderstanding.

Marie and the other nurses were sharing a taxi while a couple of other folk had come by car. Ryan refused their offers of a lift, mentally crossing his fingers that Eve would do the same. If he walked her home then he'd be able to sort this out. The last thing he wanted was her thinking that he was trying to manipulate her as her ex had done.

Eve turned to him as the last of their party disappeared and he went cold when he saw the wariness in her eyes. It seemed like a major step back after how relaxed she had been earlier. 'That's it, then. I'll see you tomorrow.'

She started to walk away but there was no way that he was letting her go without sorting this out. He hurried after her, his longer legs soon making up for the start she had.

'I'll walk you home.'

'There's no need. I'll be fine.' She didn't pause, increasing her pace so that he had to quicken his stride to keep up with her.

'I know you will but I want to talk to you about what Marie said. You do know she was joking, don't you?'

'Of course.' Although her reply was in the affirmative, her tone clearly indicated the opposite, and Ryan sighed.

'Come on, Eve. You don't honestly think that I would try to...well, *manipulate* you, do you?'

'Of course not.' She shrugged, but even though the words may have been the ones he wanted to hear, her voice said otherwise, and he felt his frustration rise.

'You do believe it. I can tell from your voice.'

They had reached the crossing and they had to wait until the lights changed. Ryan glanced at her and felt his heart sink. Her face was set, her beautiful mouth drawn into a tight line that clearly told of the strain she was under and it grieved him to know that he was responsible. Reaching out, he laid his hand on her arm, acting on instinct more than anything else. He needed to convince her that she could trust him and he needed to do it now.

'Don't!' She snatched her arm away. Spinning round, she went to step off the pavement at the same moment as a car raced through the lights, which were on red.

'Eve! No!' Ryan hooked his arm around her waist and hauled her back just in time. He could feel her trembling but he was trembling too. Turning her round, he bent so he could look into her eyes. 'You could have been killed then, do you understand that?'

'Yes!' Her eyes blazed into his. 'It might have been the best thing that could have happened, too.'

'Don't say that!' He gripped her arms, held her so that she couldn't escape, couldn't place herself in danger again. Maybe he was handling this very badly but he had to make it clear how wrong she was. 'You have everything to live for, Eve. Can't you see that?'

'No, I can't.' Tears welled to her eyes. 'If you want the truth, I can't see any point in my being here if it means me having to feel like this.'

'But you won't feel like this for ever.' His tone gentled, the need to comfort her, to soothe her, to convince her that he was right superseding everything else. Nothing mattered more than making Eve see that she had a future to look forward to. So he needed to remain detached—so what? He had obligations to his brother—what did they matter? Convincing Eve he was right far outweighed everything else.

'One day you'll look back on what's happened and it won't hurt. You'll be able to put it down to experience, see it as part of becoming the person you are.' His hands smoothed down her arms, feeling the tension that made her muscles quiver, and he was filled with fear for her. He had to make her understand that even the worst experiences could have positive results.

'You'll be happy, Eve. You'll meet someone who treats you as you deserve to be treated, fall in love, get married and have a family. You have all that ahead of you and it's far too much to turn your back on. All you need to do is believe, Eve. It will happen. I promise you that because I'll make sure it does!'

CHAPTER SIX

'THAT TEA'S COLD. Do you want me to make you a fresh cup?'

Eve jumped. Glancing up, she sighed when she saw the concern on Ryan's face. He had insisted on walking her home and coming in with her and she simply hadn't had the strength to argue with him. What had happened in the street had shaken her. Even in her darkest moments she had never considered ending her life. She hadn't really considered it tonight so why had she said that? Had it been a cry for help? Was that what she wanted, for Ryan to help her put her life back together? But surely it would only complicate matters even more if she came to rely on him. Ryan didn't *do* commitment. He hadn't done it when she'd known him before and, from what she had gleaned since she'd been at Dalverston, he still avoided it. Maybe he did want to help her but getting hung up on the idea that he might want to be more than a friend to her would be a mistake.

Eve shrugged off that thought. She wasn't looking for romance so there was no point going down that route. She dredged up a smile, feeling guilty for causing him so much distress. 'Please. I can't stand tepid tea.'

'Don't I know it!' He grinned as he went to the kettle. 'You were a real prima donna when it came to your tea.'

'I beg your pardon?' Eve stared at him in surprise and he laughed.

'Come on, you know you were. How many times did I make you a cuppa when we were on nights and you refused to drink it?' He rolled his eyes. 'In the end I gave up and let you make it yourself. It was less expensive that way. I didn't end up pouring umpteen cups of perfectly good tea down the drain!'

'Your idea of the perfect cup of tea obviously differs from mine,' she retorted. 'Anyway, you can talk. You were a bit of a diva yourself when it came to your coffee.' She mimicked his deeper tones. 'It's too strong, too weak, too hot, too sweet—the complaints were endless!'

'*Moi! A diva?* Why, that's so untrue, it's laughable.' He folded his arms across his chest. 'I've always been a model of restraint, I'll have you know. Having a hissy fit—or whatever the male equivalent is—isn't in my nature. I couldn't be a diva even if I tried!'

'Oh, no?' Eve hooted with laughter. 'What about that time you refused to sample those cakes one of the patients brought in for us? If that wasn't *diva-ish* behaviour, I don't know what is.'

'You mean the cakes that were liberally coated with cat hair? The ones that had a furry grey film stuck to the icing?' He shook his head. 'That wasn't me being a diva—it was common sense. No way was I going to eat them and end up coughing up fur balls!'

Eve laughed as he pulled a disgusted face. It was good to remember the fun they'd had. From the moment they had met there had been real rapport between them. Ryan had been the big brother she had always longed for...or that's what she had told herself.

She sighed. She had never thought about Ryan in romantic terms before that kiss and she couldn't understand why. He was good-looking and personable, kind and great fun too. He had ticked so many boxes that it seemed strange that she had never considered him as boyfriend material before that night. Why not? Had it anything to do with the fact that he'd made it clear he wasn't looking for commitment?

Although she'd been ambitious, she had always wanted to meet the right man and fall in love. She had never seen marriage as an obstacle that would prevent her having a career because of her mother. Elizabeth Pascoe was a high-flying barrister who had balanced the demands of motherhood and career in a way that had made her daughter believe it was possible to do both successfully.

Her father had helped of course. James Pascoe, a leading industrialist, had supported his wife every step of the way so that Eve had grown up with a *can-do* mentality. She'd expected to have a fulfilling career and a happy home life. It had been a given, something she had taken for granted. However, she'd realised that for it to work, she would have to find someone who was as committed to the relationship as her, and

Ryan hadn't fulfilled that criterion. He hadn't ticked that one important box.

'Here you go. Hot, not too sweet and just a dash of milk.' He placed a fresh mug of tea in front of her. Picking up a teaspoon, he carefully stirred it. 'And stirred in an anti-clockwise direction too.'

'Thank you.' Eve forced herself to smile, although it was a shock to discover how little had stood in the way of her and Ryan becoming more than friends. With the benefit of hindsight, she knew that he had found her attractive too so why had he never acted upon his feelings? Had he realised that he couldn't meet her requirements or had something else stopped him? All of a sudden she needed to know.

'When we knew each other before there was never any hint of romance between us, was there?'

'No. We were always friends.' He sat down, cradling his cup between his hands, hands that looked so big and strong and so utterly dependable that Eve felt a rush of emotions assail her. She wanted to reach out and hold his hand, have him hold hers too. The world would seem like a far less scary place if Ryan was holding her hand.

'Why?' She shrugged when he looked up, knowing that she couldn't dwell on that thought. She could see the wariness in his eyes and it intrigued her. Ryan obviously wasn't comfortable with the question but why not? 'Didn't you fancy me—was that it?'

'No. It wasn't that.'

He stared into his cup and Eve held her breath. She could tell that he was debating what to say and prayed that he would tell her the truth. For some reason it seemed important that he didn't lie about this.

'I suppose the truthful answer is that I was scared.' He looked up and her heart began to race when she saw the expression on his face. There wasn't a doubt in her mind that he was telling her the truth and all of a sudden she wasn't sure if she wanted to hear it. Once the truth was out, it couldn't be hidden away: it would have to be faced.

Ryan's palms were damp. Although lying to Eve was out of the question, he couldn't tell her the whole truth. If he told Eve why he had sworn he wouldn't marry, she might tell him that he was wrong and he couldn't afford to listen to her arguments, definitely couldn't allow himself to be swayed by them as might very well happen. He knew what he had to do and it was more important than ever that he stuck to it.

'I knew that if we did have an affair, it would be impossible to do what I had to do,' he said, his voice grating because it was hard to keep control of his emotions.

'And what did you have to do?'

'Raise money in Scott's name and make sure that other families wouldn't have to go through what mine went through.' He shrugged. 'I didn't have time for a relationship. I still don't, in fact.'

'I see. Is that why you were so distant after you kissed me that night?'

'Yes. I knew it would be wrong to move our relationship in a different direction so I decided it was better if I stayed away from you.'

'I see. But surely your brother wouldn't have wanted you to put your life on hold because of him?'

It was something Ryan had thought about many times, but it always came back to the same thing: how could he fall in love and get married when he could never risk having a family?

'Probably not but it's something *I* need to do.' He grimaced. 'When Scott first died, I went a little crazy and did all sorts of stupid things. I suppose I was tempting fate, challenging it to do its worst to me as it had done to my brother.' He sighed. 'Fortunately, I got it out of my system before anything awful happened. My parents had started fundraising by then and I got involved as well. It helped to have something to focus on. Maybe things will change in the future—who knows? But at the moment it's important to me that I do what I can to raise money for those defibrillators.'

'It's a very worthy cause,' she said softly, and Ryan felt worse than ever when he heard the approval in her voice. However, short of making a full confession, there was little he could do.

He stood up, suddenly anxious to bring the evening to an end. A lot had happened tonight and he needed to go home and regroup. Eve was right—he had been attracted to her in the past, just as he was attracted to her now, but he wouldn't do anything about it once again. She deserved so much more than he could give her: a happy marriage; a loving family; all the things a woman needed. He was no use to her as a lover but he could help her as a friend.

It was a small sop to know that, so small that it barely mopped up the edges of the pain as he took his leave. As he made his way home, Ryan couldn't help imagining how different his life would be if there weren't all these restrictions. Maybe Eve wasn't ready for another relationship yet but he could wait. And when she was ready...

His head reeled as pictures came flooding in, pictures of him and Eve doing what lovers did best. The thought of kissing her, caressing her, running his hands over her made him shudder with longing. How he ached to touch her, yearned to feel her body soft and pliant under his. He'd made love to a lot of women, although not as many as people believed, but making love to Eve would be very different. Special. In the past it had been a purely physical experience but with Eve his mind as well as his body would be engaged. Nothing would ever match it. Nothing could better it. It would be the most wonderful, most meaningful experience he'd ever had.

Only it was never going to happen. Never in a million years!

Ryan stopped dead. He had to. He simply couldn't walk when he could no longer breathe. He felt so empty, empty and alone, and it was the worst feeling ever. Without Eve in his life he would have nothing, but having her would mean she had even less. He couldn't do that to her, couldn't take away the future she was trying so desperately to reclaim. If he cared about her at all then he had to help her put her life back together. And let her go.

Eve finished seeing Daisy Martin and her parents out of the unit. The little girl was much better and had been discharged. She waved as the family stepped into the lift, mentally crossing her fingers that she wouldn't see them again soon. Daisy had been through a lot and she deserved a run of good health.

'Was that the Martins leaving?'

Eve looked round when Ryan came to join her. He had been the same as he always was, considerate and caring with the patients, and fun with the staff. Nevertheless, she had noticed a change in him since the night he had walked her home and it troubled her. She hated to think that he was worrying about her when there was no need. Since hitting an all-time low that night, she had felt much better, more positive and in control. It felt as though she had turned a corner and it was a wonderful feeling, so wonderful that she decided to share it with him. Maybe it would make him feel better too.

'Yes. Apparently, they're hoping to go over to Jamaica to visit Daisy's grandmother. They asked me what I thought and I told them I thought it was a great idea. The warmth will do wonders for Daisy's condition.'

'It will.' Ryan grinned at her. 'I wouldn't mind a couple of weeks in the sun either. It was bitter on the hills last night when I went out running.'

'When are you planning on doing this challenge?' Eve asked as they made their way to the office.

'Easter weekend.'

'But that's the end of this week!'

'Don't remind me.' He grimaced as he typed his password into the computer. 'I was puffing like an old steam engine when I got home last night. It doesn't bode well for my chances of completing this challenge.'

'Oh, I'm sure you'll manage,' she said encouragingly, but he raised a sceptical brow.

'Hmm, we'll see.'

He turned his attention to the screen, not giving her a chance to say anything else. Eve decided it could wait until later so after she had found the file she needed she headed for the door. She paused when she heard him curse.

'Damn! I don't believe it.'

'Something wrong?' Eve asked, glancing back.

'Too right there is. I've just had an email from Harry Summers to say that he won't be able to make it this weekend after all. It appears he tripped over in A and E last night and strained a tendon.' He groaned. 'I don't know what we're going to do now. We won't be able to go unless we can find someone to replace him.'

'Because of losing his sponsorship money?' Eve queried.

'No. Harry had agreed to act as our medic. We have to take someone along who isn't actually involved in the climb in case anyone gets injured.'

'Is that really necessary? I mean, everyone's medically trained.'

'Yes, they are. But our main sponsor insisted that we take someone along purely to deal with any injuries. I think they're worried in case they get sued if something happens,' he added dryly.

'Seems highly unlikely to me but I suppose you have to go along with what they want. I take it that they've pledged a lot of money?'

'Five thousand pounds, plus another five if we do some publicity for them afterwards.'

'That is a lot! I can see why you don't want to lose it.'

'Exactly. So now I need to find someone willing to give up their weekend...' He stopped and stared at her. 'You're not working over Easter, are you, Eve?'

'No,' she said slowly, because she had a nasty suspicion that she knew what was coming.

'In that case, will you come along? You'd be doing me a huge favour. At this late stage it's doubtful if I can find anyone willing to give up their weekend, which means I'll have to call it off, and that would be a disaster. So will you, Eve? Please?'

CHAPTER SEVEN

SIX O'CLOCK SATURDAY morning and it was freezing. Eve stamped her feet, hoping to generate some feeling in her numb toes. Ryan had told her to wear warm clothing and she'd thought she had followed his brief but apparently not. She'd end up with pneumonia at this rate!

The sound of an engine made her look round and she sighed in relief when she saw a minibus turning into the road. Ryan was picking her up first and then going to collect the rest of the party. At least she'd be able to thaw out once she was on the bus.

He drew up beside her, grinning as he climbed out of the driving seat. 'All ready for the off?' he asked, picking up her holdall.

'Too right.' Eve left him to toss her bag into the back and climbed aboard, shivering when she was assailed by a blast of warm air. 'If I'd had to stand there much longer, I'd have turned to ice,' she said as he got back into the cab. 'It's freezing this morning.'

'It is cold for April,' he agreed as he started the engine. He pulled away from the kerb then glanced at her, frowning as he took stock of what she was wearing. 'Haven't you anything warmer than that jacket?'

''Fraid not.' Eve huddled into the seat, soaking up the warmth like a sponge soaking up water. 'There wasn't any need for warm clothing where I was living before and I haven't had chance to buy much since I came back. This is the warmest coat I own.'

'Well, it definitely won't be warm enough where we're going.' Ryan checked his mirrors then made a U-turn.

Eve frowned. 'What are you doing?'

'Getting you some warm clothes to wear, of course.' He smiled at her. 'We can't have our replacement medic going down with frostbite, can we?'

Eve laughed, although she couldn't help the flutter her heart gave when she saw the concern in his eyes. Ryan cared about her in so many different ways and it showed. It didn't seem wise to say anything, however, so she shrugged. 'I doubt if you'll find any shops open at this hour of the day.'

'Oh, we're not going shopping,' he assured her, turning down a side street lined with beautiful old Victorian houses. He drew up outside the end one and switched off the engine. 'We're going to raid my mum's wardrobe. It'll be a lot cheaper, believe me.'

He jumped down from the bus before Eve could protest. She followed more slowly, unsure how she felt about the idea. It wasn't the thought of wearing someone else's clothes that bothered her but how it might appear. She didn't want people thinking that she and Ryan were an item.

Did she?

Eve bit her lip as she followed him up the path. He had his own key and let them in then headed along the hall. She trailed after him, trying to make sense of the emotions swirling around inside her. Whilst she didn't need any more complications in her life, she couldn't put her hand on her heart and swear that she hated the idea of people thinking she and Ryan were a couple. She didn't hate it at all, not even a little bit, and it was scary to admit it, scarier still to realise how tempting it actually was to turn fiction into fact. But would she be doing it for the right reasons? Because she wanted to be with Ryan? Or was it because it would make her feel normal to have a handsome boyfriend? She would be like everyone else then and no longer a victim.

'Ryan! What are you doing here at this hour of the morning?'

Eve jumped when she heard a woman's voice. She paused in the doorway, overcome by shyness. The woman sitting at the table had to be Ryan's mother—there was no mistaking the resemblance. She suddenly spotted Eve and stood up, smiling warmly as she came over to her.

'Hello. You must be Eve. Ryan told me that you'd agreed to go along on his latest jaunt and help out.'

'I...ahem...yes, that's right.' Eve returned her smile, although she felt a little overwhelmed by the warmth of the greeting. She couldn't help wondering what else Ryan had told his mother before she drove the thought from her mind. Ryan wouldn't betray her confidence; it wasn't in his nature.

'We can't stop, Mum,' he said, interrupting them.

'We're supposed to be picking up the others but we've hit a bit of a snag. Eve hasn't any really warm clothing and I was wondering if she could borrow some of yours.'

'Of course she can.' Patricia Sullivan immediately turned her mind to the problem as she beckoned Eve to follow her. 'Let's see what we can find, my dear.'

'Are you sure you don't mind,' Eve protested as Patricia led the way upstairs. 'I mean, it's a bit of a cheek to turn up like this and ask to borrow your clothes.'

'Nonsense! Of course I don't mind,' Patricia declared, cutting her off. She opened the door to what was obviously a guest bedroom and went straight to the wardrobe. 'I'm only too happy to help. Ryan puts so much time and effort into his fundraising and it's good to be able to do my bit.'

She began taking clothes out of the wardrobe and laying them on the bed. Eve looked at the growing pile and gulped. 'I don't think I need that amount. We're only going to be away for a few days.'

'You need to take a couple of extra things in case you get wet,' Patricia told her firmly. 'You don't want to end up with pneumonia, do you?'

'Definitely not.' Eve laughed because it was exactly what she had thought too. It seemed that she was in tune with Ryan's mother as well as with Ryan himself.

It was an unsettling thought mainly because it hinted at an intimacy she couldn't afford to foster. She helped Patricia pack the clothes into a holdall and insisted on carrying it downstairs. Ryan grinned as he took the bag from her.

'It looks as though Mum has come up trumps as usual.'

'She has. And it's very kind of her too.' Eve turned to the older woman and on a sudden impulse kissed her on the cheek. 'Thank you so much. It's really kind of you to lend me all these things.'

'I'm happy to help, my dear.' Patricia gave her a hug and amazingly Eve didn't feel at all panicky about it. It was such a huge step in the right direction that she could barely speak when Ryan told her he'd put the bag in the minibus.

Eve went to follow him, pausing when Patricia said softly, 'Look after him, Eve. I know he gives the impression that he can deal with anything life throws at him, but underneath he's still hurting. Losing his brother like that was a terrible experience for him and I only pray that one day he'll be able to put it behind him.'

'I'll do my best,' Eve said quietly, feeling a lump come to her throat.

'Thank you.'

Patricia hugged her again then waved them off. Eve waved back, deeply moved by what the older woman had said. Up till now it had been all about her: her experiences with Damien; her need to put her life back together. Now she could see that she could help Ryan too and it was uplifting to know that she had something to offer him, that it needn't be all one-sided. It could be beneficial to both of them to rekindle their... *friendship*.

A shiver passed through her as her mind faltered on the word. Although it was enough for now, she had a feeling it wouldn't be enough for ever. Not for her anyhow. As for Ryan, well, that was an entirely different matter. She had no idea how he felt.

They collected the rest of the team and set off, heading north. Ryan had decided it would be best if they completed as much of the challenge as possible in daylight so climbing Ben Nevis was first on the agenda. Marie's partner, Steve, had volunteered to act as their driver, which meant he was free to do whatever he wanted. He had been intending to go over their route again, double-checking the timings, but his mind kept wandering. Eve had behaved so naturally with his mother and he couldn't help wondering if it was a sign that she was on the road to recovery. He hoped so and not just for her sake either. Knowing that Eve was getting over all the dreadful things that had happened to her would make him feel much better too.

'So what's the plan when we reach Fort William?'

Eve leant over to look at the notes he'd made and Ryan did his best to bring his mind back on course. Although he sensed there'd been a definite improvement, he didn't intend to remark on it, especially when someone might overhear. Eve obviously wanted to keep her past to herself and he appreciated that.

'We're booked into a guest house for the night so we'll drive straight there and check that everyone has what they need,' he explained. 'If anyone's forgotten something vital there'll be time to go to the shops and buy it.'

'What sort of equipment do you need for a trip like this?' Eve asked, frowning thoughtfully.

'Hats, gloves, waterproofs, spare socks, plasters, survival blankets,' he rattled off, trying not to get hung up on the idea of how much he would love to smooth away those tiny furrows marring her brow. He took a deep breath, steering his mind away from that beguiling thought. 'I printed out a list of items that we should have with us off the Three Peaks Challenge website. It's pretty comprehensive,' he added, loath to stop talking when his thoughts were so tempted to return to a different topic. 'So we've gone with that. It seemed easier.'

'And safer,' she pointed out.

'That too,' he agreed, relieved when she smiled and the frown disappeared. Sadly, his relief didn't last, however, as he found himself taking stock once more.

She looked so pretty when she smiled, he thought, and sighed as he found himself wishing that he could make her smile more often. Although he wanted to help her, he didn't want her to become too attached to him, to save her smiles only for him. He had to remember that at the end of the day he had nothing to offer her. It was a depressing thought and he was glad when Marie interrupted and asked how long it would take them to reach the summit of Ben Nevis, the highest mountain in Scotland and the first of the peaks they were to climb.

'It's roughly a five-hour round trip,' Ryan explained, turning round so that he could look at her. His right thigh brushed against Eve's and he gritted his teeth but he could feel a wave of heat flowing from his thigh and filling his entire body with fire. He bit back a groan. How in heaven's name was he going to survive the next few hours when the slightest touch could cause this reaction.

'So what time do we need to set off?' Marie continued, oblivious to what was happening.

'Four p.m. We need to be back down by nine as we have a six-hour drive ahead of us to reach Scafell.' Ryan shifted slightly, deliberately putting some space between them in the hope that it would help. It did, although not as much as he would have liked. It still felt as though his body was burning up and it was unnerving not to be able to do anything about it. He hurried on. 'It may seem daft to drive past Scafell and head to Scotland but everyone agrees it's the best route. This way we get the highest mountain out of the way while we're still fresh.'

'Makes sense, although whether I'll still think that after I've climbed it is another matter,' Marie observed dryly.

Ryan laughed as he turned around. It was only natural that Marie should have concerns. He had them too, lots, in fact. Although he tried to keep fit, pressure of work made it impossible to keep on top of his training. He would hate to think that he might let the team down. He would hate to let Eve down too.

He sighed as he glanced at her. She had her eyes closed, although he could tell she wasn't asleep. Was she finding it as much of a strain as he was to share a seat? But why? Because coming into contact with any man alarmed her or because it was him specifically? Was Eve as aware of him as he was of her?

Ryan's heart sank. He knew it was true and it was the last thing he wanted. It simply wouldn't be right

to use the attraction Eve felt for him when it couldn't
lead anywhere. He closed his eyes, overwhelmed by
a feeling of despair. Although he knew what he had
to do, it wasn't easy when his head and his heart were
pulling him in opposite directions. If he followed his
heart, he would woo Eve, encourage her, and relish
every moment they spent together. If his heart had its
way he would find himself so deeply involved with
her that he wouldn't *want* to break free!

He took a deep breath and used it to shore up his
defences. He knew what he had to do and he would
do it too.

They were booked into a guest house on the outskirts
of Fort William. Eve followed Ryan as he led the way
inside. The owner, a pleasant-faced woman in her six-
ties called Mrs Mackinnon, came to greet them.

'You must be the party of doctors and nurses,' she
declared, opening the old-fashioned guest register.

'That's right.' Ryan made the introductions while
they signed in.

'It's nice to meet you all,' Mrs Mackinnon said,
taking some keys out of a drawer. She handed them
to Ryan. 'I'll leave you to sort yourselves out. There's
tea and coffee in the rooms so help yourselves. There's
also a list of local pubs and restaurants if you plan on
eating out tonight. Breakfast is served from seven a.m.
till nine, although I can make it earlier if you'd prefer.'

'Seven o'clock will be fine,' Ryan assured her.

Mrs Mackinnon left and they split into pairs. Marie
and Steve were sharing a room, of course, as were
Penny Groves and Tamsin Brown, two of the nurses

on Paeds. Jack Williams and Owen Archer, both registrars, were also doubling up. That left her and Ryan. Eve felt her heart turn over at the thought of sharing a room with him. He obviously realised her dilemma because he went and knocked on the door through which Mrs Mackinnon had disappeared.

'Do you have another room we can use?' he asked when she answered. 'One of our group had to drop out and Eve has come along as his replacement. I'm sure she'd prefer a room of her own.'

'Oh, dear, I'm so sorry but I don't have another room. I only have five guest rooms and they're all booked for the night.' She turned to Eve. 'You could try one of the other guest houses, dear, but I doubt they'll have any rooms available either, with it being Easter.'

'I…erm…it's all right. We'll work something out. Maybe one of the others will swop with me,' Eve said, thinking how unlikely that was.

Penny and Tamsin were unlikely to want to share with Ryan and as for Marie and Steve…well, it didn't seem fair to ask them. Marie had mentioned several times how much she was looking forward to this trip as it meant that she and Steve could spend some time alone together. As the parents of eight-year-old twin girls, enjoying a couple of nights on their own was a rare treat. Eve bit her lip as she went outside to fetch her bag. She had no idea what she was going to do.

'I'll sleep in the bus and you can have the room,' Ryan said as he joined her. He shook his head when she started to protest. 'No, it's only fair. After all, you're doing me a favour, Eve, so why should you be inconvenienced? I'll be perfectly comfortable in the bus.'

Eve doubted it. She couldn't imagine that Ryan would get much sleep if he had to use the seats as a bed. He was so tall that his feet would dangle over the end for starters. She was about to point that out when Penny appeared, looking decidedly sheepish.

'You won't believe it but I've only forgotten my walking boots,' she explained, pulling a face.

Ryan laughed. 'It's easily done. What do you want to do? I can run you into town to see if you can find another pair.'

'Would you mind?' Penny perked up. She glanced round, her smile widening when she saw Jack. 'Ryan's offered to run me into town to buy some boots—do you want to come?'

'Yeah. Great.'

Jack returned her smile and Eve could tell that it wasn't the thought of the outing that was making him look so cheerful. There was obviously something going on between him and Penny.

For some reason the thought was depressing. It never normally bothered her when she saw couples who were obviously happy to be with one another but today it did. When Ryan asked her if she wanted to tag along for the ride, she declined. It wouldn't help to play gooseberry; it would only make her feel worse, although if she and Ryan were together that would be a different matter.

Eve cut short that thought and picked up her bag. She took it up to her room and started to unpack: toiletries, clean undies, a sweater to wear that night for dinner. She sighed as she laid the sweater on the bed because there was no point pretending. The thought of herself and Ryan being a couple was a far more attractive prospect than she would have believed. She could imagine them going out and having fun together. She could imagine them *staying in* and having fun too!

Heat flowed through her and it shocked her that she didn't find the prospect of intimacy as terrifying as it had been. Did it mean that she was over the worst? She hoped so. She wanted to be able to look forward to a life untainted by past experiences and make plans for the future. Would Ryan be part of that future? Although he'd definitely kick-started the healing process—she was absolutely sure about that—whether he would play a role in her future was another matter.

Picking up her toilet bag, Eve went into the bathroom and arranged everything neatly on the shelf. It was better to focus on practicalities than dream about a future that might never materialise. That was the mistake she'd made with Damien; she had imagined the wonderful life they would have and had held onto the dream long after it had become clear that it wasn't going to happen. She would be a fool to do it again and end up with her life in tatters once more.

CHAPTER EIGHT

THEY DECIDED TO eat at the local pub that night. It was just a short walk from the guest house, which saved them having to drive. It was still very cold, much colder than Ryan had expected, and he was a little concerned about the impact it could have on their plans. However, he decided not to say anything in case it spoiled the evening. If the guide he'd hired had any reservations about them making the climb, they would call it off and hope that their sponsors would support them if they tried again later in the year.

'Right, so what's it to be, folks? The first round's on me.' He smiled around the table, trying not to let his gaze linger on Eve, but it was impossible when she looked so lovely. His heart picked up its beat as he drank in every detail from the fluffy peach sweater that just hinted at the soft curves beneath to the well-worn jeans that encased her shapely legs. She'd left her hair loose again and his hands clenched as he fought to resist the urge to feel how silky it was. Everything about her was soft, gentle, womanly, and despite his best efforts, he couldn't help responding.

'*Hello!* Come in, Ryan. Are you receiving me?'

Ryan jumped when Marie tapped him none too gently on the arm. 'Sorry! Just having a senior moment,' he said hastily, using the first excuse that came to mind.

'Hmm, is that what it was?' Marie retorted, giving him an old-fashioned look. She glanced pointedly at Eve and Ryan swallowed his groan.

If Marie had realised why he was so distracted, it wouldn't be long before Eve reached the same conclusion. The thought was more than he could handle and he swiftly changed the subject. 'So what's it to be, then? Marie, you go first as you're obviously in dire need of alcoholic refreshment.'

He made a note of their orders and went to the bar. The pretty young waitress offered to bring their drinks over so he picked up a handful of menus and took them back to the table. 'Here you go. See what you fancy.'

He handed Eve a menu, feeling his heart leap when she smiled at him. Sitting down, he focused diligently on the dishes on offer. It was foolish to imagine that Eve had saved her warmest smile for him. After all, she had smiled just as warmly at Jack and Owen.

The thought was like a dousing of cold water and it soon rid him of any more fanciful notions. Ryan decided what he wanted and gave his order to the waitress when she brought their drinks across, responding automatically when she started flirting with him. Tamsin chuckled as the girl reluctantly left.

'Not lost the old Sullivan magic, eh, Ryan?' She turned to Jack and Owen. 'I hope you guys are taking note of how it's done. It could stand you in good stead in the future!'

Everyone laughed, Ryan included, although it was hard to drum up any real amusement. He glanced at Eve and felt his heart sink. Even though she was laughing, he had a feeling that she didn't find it funny. Why not? Because it reminded her of how her ex had behaved? He'd been a flirt, too, although Ryan hated to think that he had anything in common with the other man. Nevertheless, it could well appear that way to Eve.

The thought plagued him all through dinner. Although the food was good, he barely noticed what he ate. It was a relief when everyone finished and decided to return to the guest house. Eve went on ahead with Tamsin and Marie so he didn't get the chance to say anything to her. Penny and Jack were trailing behind and he knew they'd be the butt of a lot of good-natured teasing in the morning, not that it would bother them.

He sighed as he found himself wishing that Eve had reached that point, that any comments about her and a man would be taken in good part and not trigger a load of terrible memories. Until that happened, she would never be truly free of the past and it hurt to know that it could be years before it happened. Eve didn't deserve any of this. She really didn't!

They reached the guest house and Ryan hung back, not wanting the others to know that he planned to sleep on the bus when it would invite a lot of awkward questions. He waited until Penny and Jack were safely inside before he unlocked the bus, grimacing when he was greeted by a blast of chilly air. It wouldn't have been his first choice to sleep in here but he'd survive. And it was a lot better than upsetting Eve.

Eve couldn't sleep. She tossed and turned for over an hour but it was no use; she couldn't stop thinking about Ryan sleeping on the bus. It was bitterly cold and he'd be frozen if he had to spend the night out there. It wasn't fair when he was setting off on this challenge the following day. He needed a good night's sleep otherwise he might not make it back safely.

The thought had her leaping out of bed. Dragging her coat over her pyjamas, she opened the door. It was almost midnight and there was no sound from the other bedrooms as she crept along the landing. Everyone was making sure they got a good night's rest in readiness for the task ahead and the thought reinforced her feeling that it was wrong to allow Ryan to camp out on the bus. If he had to drop out because he was exhausted, she would never forgive herself!

Eve ran downstairs and unlocked the front door. She could see a light on in the minibus and sighed. Obviously, Ryan wasn't asleep and she felt guiltier than ever. Opening the door, she climbed into the bus and spotted him lying curled up across a row of seats. He was still wearing his clothes and from the look of it several other layers too in an attempt to ward off the cold. He sat up when he heard her come in and she saw the surprise on his face.

'Eve! What is it? Has something happened?'

'No. I couldn't sleep for worrying about you being out here,' she told him bluntly. 'It's not fair, Ryan.

You need a good night's sleep if you're to complete this challenge.'

'I'm fine,' he assured her, but she didn't believe him.

'So why aren't you asleep? Why are you lying there wide awake at this hour?' She glared at him. 'I'll tell you why. You can't sleep because it's freezing cold in here. It's ridiculous, Ryan, really it is.'

'So what do you suggest? That we swop places?' He shook his head. 'No way. You're not spending the night out here, Eve. I won't let you.'

'In that case, we shall have to act like grown-ups and share.'

'I beg your pardon?'

He sounded so shocked that Eve experienced a momentary doubt before she dismissed it. It was the only sensible solution. She and Ryan would have to share the room and that was that.

'You heard me. We'll share the room. It's a twin so it's not like we'll be in the same bed.' She swung round before he could say anything. 'I'll leave the door on the latch for you.'

Eve made her way back inside, refusing to allow the pictures that were clamouring to break free to fill her mind. She and Ryan were friends and if they couldn't share a room for the night then it was a sorry state of affairs. She hurried back to the bedroom, taking off her coat and climbing into one of the twin beds. She heard a floorboard creak as someone came along the landing then a pause before the door opened and Ryan appeared.

'Are you absolutely sure about this, Eve?'

Eve could hear the indecision in his voice and was overwhelmed by misgivings all of a sudden. She had never envisaged sharing a room with him or any other man. The very idea had terrified her, in fact. However, if she didn't do this, and Ryan failed to complete the challenge, she would always regret it.

'Of course I'm sure,' she said with as much confidence as she could muster. 'I wouldn't have suggested it otherwise.'

'In that case, thanks.'

He closed the door and took off his coat and hung it on the hook. A fleece jacket came next and a sweater until he was down to a short-sleeved T-shirt. Eve took one look at the muscular width of his back and gulped. It was a long time since she'd been in this position, shut up in a bedroom with a man wearing only a minimal amount of clothing!

Rolling onto her side, she closed her eyes, deciding it would be easier not to watch. However, with her vision impaired, her other senses came into play. There was a soft thud as Ryan kicked off his trainers, followed by the rustle of denim as he removed his jeans, and she bit back a groan. It was even worse with her eyes closed because now her imagination was filling in the gaps. Would he strip completely and sleep in the buff? A lot of men preferred not to wear any clothing in bed so was Ryan one of them?

Her mind raced off with the thought, conjuring up a picture of him stark naked, and she buried her face in the pillow. All she could see in her mind's eye was his tall figure in all its splendour—those broad shoulders and well-muscled chest, the narrow hips and muscular thighs…

'Night-night, Eve, sleep tight. Mind the bugs don't bite, as my mum used to say when we were kids.'

There was a hint of laughter in his voice and Eve's face flamed. She was glad of the pillow because it hid her embarrassment. Had Ryan guessed what she was thinking? Probably!

The thought was more than she could bear. Reaching out, she switched off the lamp, plunging the room into darkness. She wasn't sure which was worse, the fact that her treacherous imagination had seen fit to conjure up that picture of him or that he had guessed. Curling up into a tight little ball, she tried to ignore the heat that was flowing through her veins. She needed to sleep if only to stop her imagination running riot.

Cotton rustled, a pillow was thumped, and Eve realised it wasn't going to happen. There was no way that she'd be able to sleep with Ryan lying a couple of feet away from her. She groaned softly and heard him sigh.

'This isn't going to work, is it, Eve? It was madness to think it would.' She heard the bed creak as he got up. 'I'm going back to the bus. That way at least one of us will get some sleep.'

'No, don't!' Eve sat up and switched on the lamp. She gulped as she was met by the sight of his nearly naked body. Contrary to what she had thought, he was wearing some clothes. However, the black jersey trunks left very little to the imagination. She looked up, keeping her eyes focused on his face. 'I won't let you sleep on the bus. It isn't fair.'

'Neither is this.' He ran his hands through his hair and she could tell how frustrated he felt, and no wonder. It had been her decision to invite him to share the room after all.

'I'm sorry. It's just that I haven't shared a room with anyone since...well...' She broke off, unable to continue.

'I understand, Eve, really I do.' He came and sat down on the edge of her bed and his expression was so gentle that it brought tears to her eyes. It had been a long time since anyone had cared about her feelings this much. He sighed softly. 'Don't cry, Eve. I can't bear to know that I've upset you.'

'You haven't. It's this situation. I hate it that I feel this way yet I can't seem to stop.'

'But you're getting better.' He looked into her eyes. 'You kissed my mum this morning, didn't you? That was a real step forward.'

'Yes, it was,' she agreed slowly. 'I would *never* have done that a couple of weeks ago.'

'Exactly.' Reaching out, he wiped away her tears with his fingers and smiled at her. 'You're making amazing progress, Eve, and I'm really proud of you. I know you'll beat this one day and I'll be right there, cheering you on, too.'

'You're really kind, Ryan,' she said, her voice thickening with emotion. 'I don't know why you want to help me but I appreciate it.'

'I want to help because we're friends and I care about you, Eve. It's as simple as that.' He smiled at her. 'Now I have a suggestion, although I'm not sure how you'll feel about it so I want you to be honest with

me. I won't be offended if you say no but it might help
us both get some sleep.'

'What is it?' she asked cautiously.

'That we sleep together in the same bed. Not sleep
together in *that* way, obviously. I'm not suggesting
that. But if we share a bed then every time I roll over
you won't be wondering what I'm doing *and* fearing
the worst!'

He laughed and amazingly Eve laughed too. It was
so exactly what would have happened that she couldn't
helped being amused. 'Hmm, you don't do mind-
reading in your spare time, do you, Dr Sullivan?'

'How did you guess?' He sobered abruptly. 'I swear
that I won't try anything, Eve. So what do you think?
Would it help?'

'Perhaps.' She bit her lip then suddenly made up
her mind. 'Let's give a try. If it doesn't work, you can
always go back to your own bed.'

'Precisely.' He turned back the quilt and slid in beside her. 'Come on—budge up, bed-hog.'

'Who are you calling a bed-hog?' Eve demanded
as she scooted over to give him some room.

She tensed when she felt his body brush against
hers as he made himself comfortable. It was Ryan
and he would never hurt her, she reminded herself,
and after a moment managed to relax. Closing her
eyes, she let her mind drift, surprised by how comfortable she felt. Lying next to Ryan wasn't scary at
all. On the contrary, it made her feel safe and wonderfully secure. Her breath caught. It also made her
feel like *her*.

* * *

Six o'clock and the sun was streaming in through the window. Ryan stretched luxuriously. He hadn't expected to feel *this* good after a night on the bus…

His mind suddenly joined up the dots and his eyes flew open, although it took him a second to believe what he was seeing, which was the back of Eve's head. Her red-gold hair was spread across the pillow, leaving the nape of her neck exposed, and he gulped. He could imagine pressing his lips to that sweet spot, tasting the satiny warmth of her skin.

And how she would react if he did!

He bit back a groan. Eve had trusted him last night and it had been such a huge step for her that he wouldn't do anything that might cause him to lose that trust. Tossing back the quilt, he made for the bathroom. A cold shower should curtail any more such urges.

Ten minutes later, cold inside and out, he went back into the bedroom. Eve was awake and he was glad that he had appropriated the largest towel for his use. The cold water may have worked but its effects were proving to be purely temporary, unfortunately.

'Good morning, and I'm pleased to say that it looks like a really lovely morning too.' He swept open the curtains like a weather man on steroids. 'See! A perfect day to go climbing.'

'That's good news.'

She sat up and scooped back her hair, fastening a band around it to hold it back from her face, and Ryan only just managed to stop himself protesting. However, it wasn't his place to comment on her hairstyle. Friends they were and friends they had to re-main, even if his body wasn't completely enamoured with the idea.

He hurriedly picked up his holdall as parts of him that had been frozen into submission began to thaw out. 'I'll just commandeer the bathroom again while I get dressed. Won't be a sec.'

He shot through the door, closing it thankfully be-hind him. That had been a close call, although he doubted if Eve had realised why he'd made such a speedy exit. He sighed as he took fresh underwear out of the bag. He didn't want to feel this way but he couldn't help it. If it had been a purely physical re-sponse he could have dealt with it but he knew in his heart it was more than that. He was attracted to Eve not only for her looks but because of who she was—a brave, funny, caring woman who would steal his heart if he weren't careful.

Ryan took a deep breath as he dragged a clean T-shirt over his head. Somehow he had to stay strong, had to resist, *had to* protect her. The one thing he must never do was fall in love with Eve or allow her to fall in love with him when it would ruin her life all over again.

CHAPTER NINE

As soon as breakfast was finished they brought their bags downstairs and paid the bill. Eve was a little embarrassed when Ryan insisted on paying for their room and refused to let her go halves. Although she understood that he felt it was only right that he should cover her expenses when she was filling in for Harry Summers, she was aware of how it must appear to the rest of the group. Nobody had commented on them sharing a room, although she wasn't foolish enough to think it had gone unnoticed. There would be a lot of speculation about their relationship.

They started loading the minibus, which took a surprisingly long time. They worked in pairs, checking their own equipment first then getting their buddy to check it and make sure nothing was missing. Eve acted as Ryan's buddy, marking off everything on the list. Once that was done they loaded the water butts into the back. Mrs Mackinnon had allowed them to fill them up in her kitchen, although for the life of her Eve couldn't understand why they needed to take so much water with them and said so.

'You get very dehydrated at high altitudes,' Ryan

explained, closing the van doors. 'We'll each need to carry bottles of water with us and it's easier if we can fill them up from the butts.'

'Oh, I see. I must confess I did wonder if you were expecting a drought.'

Ryan laughed. 'Not in Scotland, no, although I'll have to make provision for it if I do the Sahara walk later on this year.'

'You're doing another challenge!' she exclaimed as they boarded the bus.

'I hope so.' He waited for her to slip into the row of seats and sat beside her. 'It's still not finalised, mainly because there's been some unrest in the area. Hopefully, things will calm down soon and it can go ahead.'

'I see.'

Eve felt alarm run through her. She hated the thought of Ryan putting himself in danger, although she wasn't sure if it was her place to say so. In the end she stayed silent, not that anyone noticed. Everyone was in very high spirits and talked non-stop as they drove to the Glen Nevis Visitor centre where Ryan had arranged to meet their guide. Steve had mentioned over lunch that he would return to Fort William with the minibus after they had unloaded their gear. He needed to get some sleep as he would be driving through the night. Eve wasn't sure what she was expected to do. As the team's medic, surely she should stay? As soon as they'd finished sorting out their equipment, she asked Ryan.

'It'll be best if you go back with Steve. The visitor centre closes at five p.m. at this time of the year and there's no point you hanging around in the cold.' He checked his notes. 'We're hoping to be back down by nine so you can come back and meet us then.'

'But what happens if someone has an accident?' she protested. 'There's no point my coming if I'm not around to help.'

'If anything happens, I'll phone Steve and he can bring you back.'

'You're sure your phone will work up here?' she said sceptically, glancing at the surrounding mountains.

'Some mobiles can get a signal and others can't, so if my phone won't work, someone else's probably will. Anyway, Tom Fraser, our guide, assured me that he'd be able to summon help if need be.'

'Oh, right. I see.' Eve couldn't help feeling disappointed at the thought of being of so little use and Ryan obviously realised it.

'You're not getting off as lightly as you think.' He grinned at her. 'We're expecting you and Steve to rustle up a tasty little gourmet snack for when we get back. I hope your culinary skills are up to satisfying six hungry climbers.'

'I'll do my best.' Eve laughed, appreciating the fact that he was concerned about her feelings when there were so many more important things to worry about. 'However, I should warn you that cordon bleu might be a tad beyond my capabilities. How does a pot of instant noodles grab you?'

He rolled his eyes. 'It doesn't!'

They both burst out laughing and Marie, who happened to be passing on her way to use the bathroom in the visitor's centre, grinned at them. 'Hmm, are you sure you two didn't arrange for Harry to have that accident? You look *very* cosy together, I must say.'

She carried on before either of them could say anything, not that Eve could think of very much. It was only what she had suspected after all, that the rest of the group would start speculating about her and Ryan. Ryan sighed. 'Sorry about that. Marie doesn't mean any harm but I rather think she's put two and two together and come up with ten.'

'It's only to be expected,' Eve said lightly, not wanting to cause a fuss.

'Probably. But how do you feel about it? I'd hate to think that you felt, well, uncomfortable about folk assuming we're a couple. If you do then I shall make it clear that we're not.'

'I doubt they'd believe you after last night,' she pointed out. 'We did share a room, Ryan.'

'Yes, and nothing happened.' He touched her hand and she could hear the sincerity in his voice. 'Thank you for trusting me, Eve. It meant a lot.'

'Thank you for making me trust you,' she said with equal sincerity. She looked into his eyes and all of a sudden it felt as though a huge chunk of fear had melted away. 'It meant an awful lot to me, too, Ryan.'

'I'm glad.' His eyes darkened and she knew he was going to say something, only just then a battered old vehicle drew up in the car park. A tall man with a shock of bright red hair jumped out and came over to them.

'Dr Sullivan?' he said in a soft Scottish burr. 'I'm Tom Fraser, your guide.'

The two men shook hands and immediately turned

their attention to the forthcoming climb. Eve moved away and let them get on with it. She felt very strange, sort of shivery inside, as though something momentous had happened. She bit her lip as she went back to the bus and told Steve that she would be returning to Fort William with him.

The fear that she had carried around with her for so long had suddenly lifted and it was a strange feeling not to have its weight bowing her down. She felt free for the first time in years and it was slightly scary to shake off the constraints and not have to impose all those restrictions on her life.

She glanced over her shoulder, feeling her heart jolt as her eyes alighted on Ryan. He was responsible for this change in her and she would always be grateful to him. Maybe she hadn't fully got back to being the person she had been but she was on her way and knew that one day she would find herself again. Would Ryan still be around to witness the metamorphosis, though? She hoped so, hoped for it with every scrap of her being, although she mustn't set her heart on it. Having seen the way he had flirted with that waitress, it was clear that he still enjoyed playing the field. It would be foolish to think he was ready for commitment.

She sighed. Although having Ryan around might make her life complete, it could turn out to be nothing more than a pipe dream.

It was tough going, despite the preparations they had made. Ryan could feel his calf muscles aching as he followed Tom Fraser to the summit of Ben Nevis. The rest of the group had fallen silent now, saving their breath for the climb. They finally reached the top and stopped, awed by the view that met them.

All around them lay mountains, most of them capped with snow as Ben Nevis itself was. Ryan heard everyone exclaim in amazement but he was so moved by the sight that he couldn't utter a word. These mountains had stood here for millions of years and it heightened the feeling he'd had since Scott had died of how ephemeral human life was. He found himself wishing that he could have shared this moment with his brother, stood here with him and drunk in the timeless magnificence of the view. It would have brought all their plans for the future into focus.

It was a moment of revelation, a moment that made him wonder if he was wrong to live the way he did. Even if he might pass on the gene that caused LQTS, there had to be a way around it. Other couples coped so why couldn't he? If he could accept that there might be a problem if he fathered a child and prepare for it then he could have everything he'd ever dreamed about—a woman to love and, one day, a family too.

He closed his eyes, letting his mind fill in the details. It was so easy too. He didn't want just any woman; he wanted Eve. He wanted to live with her, love her, have children with her and grow old with her too. They might even be blessed with grandkids one day and he could picture them too, see their smiling faces, hear their laughter. It was all so clear that for a moment he almost believed it could happen, before sanity returned.

He couldn't put Eve through all the stress of wondering if their child might be afflicted by this terrible condition. He couldn't expect her to live in fear if their child inherited LQTS. No woman should have to go through that ordeal and especially not Eve. Not after everything else she had been through.

Ryan turned away, his heart aching. 'OK, guys, let's get moving. We don't want to waste too much time.'

Nobody questioned his decision. They all knew that there were time restrictions if they hoped to complete the challenge. Ryan followed Tom down, telling himself it would be easier once he got off the mountain. Easier and far less emotive. It was the sheer magnificence of the setting that had set loose these feelings. He knew what he had to do and he wasn't going to change his mind. Not for any reason. Or for any one.

Eve and Steve were waiting when they got back. They had hot chocolate ready and everyone eagerly accepted a mug. Tom drank his chocolate then bid them farewell, obviously keen to get home. Eve was frying bacon on the camping stove, filling rolls with it and wrapping them in foil so they could be eaten on the bus. She handed them out while Steve dealt with the stove, stowing it safely away in its heat-proof box.

'These smell good. Thanks.' Ryan dredged up a smile but he still felt raw. It wasn't easy to shake off that moment of introspection but he had to do so. Protecting Eve was his number-one priority and nothing else mattered as much as that. He climbed onto the bus, deliberately opting to sit next to Owen for the next leg of the journey. He would never rid himself of these foolish ideas if he had to spend the next six hours sitting beside Eve.

Eve couldn't help feeling hurt when Ryan chose to sit with Owen. Had she done something wrong? she wondered as she slid into the seat next to Tamsin. She sighed, realising how silly she was being. Ryan probably wanted to discuss the next leg of the challenge with Owen and it was as simple as that.

She ate her bacon roll and then tried to sleep. Steve had switched off the interior lights and most of the party were dozing, although she knew that Ryan was awake. She could hear him moving occasionally as he tried to get comfortable. Drawing the fleece jacket around her—one that Patricia Sullivan had lent her— Eve tried to ignore the sounds but it was impossible. Every time he moved, her heart leapt or her breathing speeded up. She was just so aware of him after the thoughts she'd had that day that it was impossible to get him out of her mind.

She closed her eyes, willing herself to sleep, and dozed off only to wake with a start when the bus swerved violently. Pandemonium broke out as bags rained down from the overhead racks. Steve switched on the lights and Eve could see how shaken he looked.

'Sorry about that, guys. There's a car back there and it looks as though it's been in an accident. I had to swerve to avoid it.'

'Better take a look and see if we can help,' Ryan said immediately.

He hurried down the aisle and after a moment everyone trooped after him. Eve could see a car lying on its side in the centre of the road and went cold as she realised what might have happened if Steve hadn't reacted so quickly. Jumping down from the bus, she ran towards it. There were five people inside: a young-ish couple in the front and an older woman plus two small children in the rear. Although they could hear the children screaming, the adults weren't moving and were either unconscious or deeply shocked. Ryan im-mediately took charge.

'Steve, can you phone the emergency services and explain what's happened? You should be able to get our location off the sat nav. Tell them we'll update them as to the severity of any injuries once we've ex-amined them.'

'Will do!'

Steve ran back to the bus while Ryan and Jack at-tempted to open the car's doors. They had to climb onto the vehicle, which made it that much more dif-ficult. Jack shook his head when they failed to gain entry after a great deal of tugging.

'It's no good, the central locking must be on.'

'Bang on the window and try to rouse the driver,' Ryan instructed. He too hammered on the glass and after a couple of seconds the man looked round. 'Open the doors,' he shouted.

Eve heaved a sigh of relief when the doors were re-leased. Leaving Ryan and Jack to deal with the driver, she climbed onto the car and opened the rear door, smiling at the little boy who was strapped into a safety seat. He looked to be about two years old and was ob-viously terrified. 'It's all right, poppet. We're going to get you out and make you feel better.'

She slid her hand behind his head, gently feeling for any signs of swelling that could indicate a head trauma, and was relieved when she found nothing untoward. The child car seat appeared to have done its job and saved him from a nasty injury. The next step was to get him out of the car so she could examine him properly.

'How's he doing?' Ryan suddenly appeared beside her.

Eve looked down from her elevated position and shrugged. 'No obvious signs of head trauma but I need to get him out of this seat so I can take a proper look at him.'

'Take it really slowly,' he advised her. 'You don't want to jolt his neck and spine as you lift him out.'

'Will do.'

Eve released the safety catch and eased the child out of the seat, passing him straight to Ryan. She jumped down, nodding when Ryan put his hand under her elbow to steady her.

'Thanks. I'm going to take him back to the bus. It'll be easier to examine him in there,' she explained, trying to ignore the little flutter of awareness that had shot through her at his touch.

'Good idea.' He frowned as he glanced into the car. 'We need to get the woman out before we can examine the girl. Will you ask Steve to give me a hand? Jack and Owen are sorting out the driver and passenger and I don't want them to have to break off from what they're doing.' He lowered his voice. 'The passenger doesn't look too good, I'm afraid.'

Eve nodded, not wanting to labour the point in

front of the little boy. She carried him back to the bus and passed on Ryan's message. Marie went with her and within a very short time they had made the child comfortable on the front seat.

'I'll check him over, although I don't think he's badly injured,' Eve explained, unzipping his anorak. She tested his arms and legs for fractures then felt his tummy to see if there was any swelling that could indicate internal bleeding. He had stopped screaming now and was lying quietly while she carried out her examination, and she smiled at him.

'What a good little boy you are. Can you tell me your name, sweetheart?'

'Finlay,' he lisped.

'What a lovely name!' Eve ruffled his dark curls, feeling much happier now that she was sure he wasn't badly hurt. 'My name's Eve and this lady is called Marie. Marie's going to look after you while I go and help your sister. OK?'

Leaving Marie with the child, she ran back to the car. Ryan and Steve were attempting to lift the older woman out, no easy feat when they had to balance on the side of the vehicle. Although Eve knew that moving a casualty should be undertaken with a great deal of caution, she guessed that they were anxious to reach the little girl. The woman was lying half on top of her, which made it imperative they get her out.

They finally lifted the woman out and laid her on the ground. She was unconscious and her colour was poor. Ryan shook his head as he checked her pulse. 'Pulse is very fast. Her breathing's not good either. Can you phone Ambulance Control and warn them we have a casualty who needs immediate transfer to hospital?'

Eve helped him fit the woman with a cervical collar from the bag of medical supplies they had brought along while Steve made the call. Once that was done Ryan examined her. He frowned. 'Air intake appears restricted on the left side. It could be a haemothorax. She may have broken a rib when she fell sideways and hit the child seat. If blood is collecting in the pleural cavity, the lung could collapse so she needs monitoring.' He called Penny over and explained what he needed her to do then stood up.

'Let's get the little girl out of there. How's the boy, by the way?'

'Fine.' Eve smiled, wanting to ease some of the worry from his face. 'He managed to tell me his name, which is a good sign.'

'It is indeed.'

Ryan returned her smile and she felt warmth flow through her when she saw the tenderness in his eyes. There wasn't a doubt in her mind at that moment that he cared about her and not only as a friend either. The thought made her heart lift, filled it with all sorts of emotions so that she felt momentarily giddy before she managed to get herself in hand. This wasn't the time to be thinking about things like that but later, when they had done all they could for these people, she would return to it.

A feeling of joy swept over her as she helped him lift the little girl out of the car. Maybe it wouldn't take as long as she had feared to shake off the past. Not when she had Ryan to help her.

CHAPTER TEN

EVEN THOUGH THE emergency services had arrived remarkably quickly, they were still well over an hour behind schedule. Ryan had a last word with the paramedics, who were ferrying the driver and the children to hospital, then ran back to the bus. The two women had been airlifted out by helicopter and were already on their way. Their injuries were far more serious and the sooner they received treatment the better. Everyone was on board and he wasted no time as he told Steve they could leave.

'The police have my phone number. They're going to contact me later and take a statement,' he explained as they set off. 'They've also promised to let us know how the family's doing.'

'The driver and the kids should be fine, but as for the mother and grandmother...' Tamsin grimaced.

Ryan shrugged, trying to make light of her fears. Although the two women had been seriously injured, the younger one having sustained pelvic injuries and the older woman showing definite signs of a haemothorax, they themselves needed to remain focused if they were to complete the challenge. 'At least they're on their way to hospital so that means they have the best chance possible.'

'I guess so,' Tamsin conceded.

Ryan sighed as Tamsin slumped down in her seat. The accident had put a dampener on the day and all he could do was hope that it wouldn't affect their performance. They'd worked hard to reach a standard whereby they could attempt this challenge and it would be a huge shame if they failed.

'Cheer up. I'm sure it will be fine once we reach Scafell Pike. Everyone's still a bit shocked by what's happened but they'll soon rally.'

'Think so?' Ryan looked round, immediately feeling better when Eve smiled at him. Although he knew it was crazy, a smile from her was guaranteed to lift his spirits.

'I know so,' she replied firmly, and he laughed.

'You sound very sure of yourself. How come you're such an expert in these matters?'

'I'm not.' She shrugged. 'I just know what a great bunch of people they are. They'll perk up after they've had a rest—you'll see.'

'I hope you're right. In fact, I shall hold you to it.'

He smiled at her, loving the way her face lit up with an answering smile. That was something he remembered very clearly, that whenever he'd smiled at her she had smiled back with real warmth. She had been such a positive person back then and he found himself praying that she would be the same again one day. To have Eve back, the *old* Eve whom he had liked so much, would be marvellous. In a funny sort of a way it would feel as though he'd found a bit of himself that had been missing ever since she had disappeared from his life.

It was the first time that thought had occurred to him and it shocked him. He had missed Eve, missed her far more than he had admitted. Had he deliberately played down his feelings? Refused to admit to himself how upset he'd been when she had left?

With a sudden flash of insight he realised it was true. Eve had meant a lot to him and she could have meant even more if he hadn't been so determined to maintain his distance after that kiss they'd shared. He had known that Eve had been attracted to him too and it made him feel guilty all of a sudden to realise that if he hadn't kept her at arm's length, she might not have got involved with Damien. Eve's life could have been very different if he'd had the courage to admit how he'd felt, yet how could he have done that when it could have had such a detrimental impact on her life? Maybe she had been through a terrible ordeal with her ex but it wouldn't have turned out any better if she'd been involved with him.

The thought hit him hard. Ryan closed his eyes, trying to control the rush of emotions it aroused. He was no use to Eve; he never had been. The sooner he accepted that, the better. However, the one thing he mustn't do was to let Eve know how he felt and why. He couldn't afford to let her convince him that his fears were groundless. He knew they weren't. He knew it only too well.

They reached Scafell Pike over an hour after they had planned to arrive. Ryan was all business as he chivvied everyone off the bus and made sure they had what they needed. Eve stood to one side, not wanting to get in the way. She frowned when she heard him speak rather sharply to Penny, who had forgotten to fill her water bottle.

He seemed very uptight and she found it hard to understand what was bothering him, unless it was the thought of them not completing the challenge in time. They had just twenty-four hours to climb all three peaks and the accident had set them back. Ryan must be worried that they wouldn't make it, which would be a disaster if it meant they couldn't collect the promised sponsorship money.

'Right, we should be back here by eight-thirty.' Ryan checked his watch. 'We'll need to get a move on so can you have everything ready? Don't bother about any hot food. We'll make do with sandwiches.'

'Fine,' Eve agreed quietly. He turned to leave but she couldn't let him go like this. Although she knew how important this was to him, his safety came first. 'Take care, Ryan. I don't want to have to put you back together because you've tried to go too fast.'

'I'll be fine.'

He moved away, making it clear that he didn't welcome her advice, and Eve's face flamed. It was hard to dredge up a smile when the others wished her a cheery goodbye. Had she overstepped the mark? she wondered as she fired up the stove to make coffee for herself and Steve. Probably. Ryan had always been very independent and probably he didn't appreciate people fussing over him. However, she found it hard to believe it was that which had caused him to be so short with her. She had a feeling there was more to it than that and the thought plagued her. She didn't want to be at odds with him, especially when she didn't know what she had done wrong.

She sighed. Feeling that she was in the wrong was something that she had grown accustomed to with Damien. He'd made her feel that she was always at fault and that nothing that had happened had been down to him. It had been all part of turning her into a victim and there was no way that it was going to happen again. If she *had* upset Ryan then she would make him tell her what she had done and that would be the end of it.

By the time the party returned some four hours later, Eve was seething. She handed out the sandwiches and climbed into the bus, meaning to have it out with Ryan. However, once again he chose not to sit with her, opting to sit up front with Steve so she missed her chance. Everyone was worn out after their exertions and there was little chatter as they drove to north Wales.

Fortunately, the traffic wasn't too bad and they managed to make up some of the time they had lost but Eve knew they would be hard pressed to meet the deadline. It wasn't the right moment to broach the subject with Ryan but she promised herself that she would have it out with him later. She needed to know exactly where she stood with him.

The thought sent a shiver down her spine and she hugged her arms around herself as she watched the group depart. It was hard to believe that Ryan had become so important to her in such a short time. Why, just a week ago she had been determined to keep him at arm's length but that was no longer possible. He had become a major part of her life now and she needed his support, his kindness; needed him.

What did it mean? Was it possible that she was falling in love with him? Although she knew it was far too soon to start thinking like that, she couldn't rule it out when she felt things for him that she'd not felt for any other man.

They made it to the top of Snowdon and down again in the nick of time but only because Ryan had pushed them all to the limit. As he looked at the exhaustion on their faces, he felt guiltier than ever. These people—his friends—had given up their time to support his fundraising efforts and he'd repaid them by behaving like a slave driver.

'I don't know what to say except thank you. You've all been brilliant—there's no other word for it. Just brilliant!'

'I'd say it's been a pleasure only I'll probably get locked up for lying,' Marie retorted, groaning as she sank down on the ground and massaged her aching calf muscles. 'I'm going to be fit for nothing next week. You could find yourself running Paeds all on your own!'

Ryan laughed. 'That'll teach me to push you all so hard.' He looked round when Eve came to join them, doing his best to control his racing heart, but it was impossible. He only had to look at her and his heart raced, his breathing quickened, and as for other bits of him...

He cut short that thought, not daring to go down that route. 'Right, unless you fancy doing it all over again, I suggest we head off to the guest house. I don't know about you lot, but a long hot soak in the bath sounds like bliss to me.'

Murmurs of approval greeted the suggestion. Ryan tossed his haversack into the back of the bus and went to shut the doors, pausing when he heard someone calling his name. Glancing round, he gasped when he saw the couple hurrying towards him. The last time he'd seen Sarah and David had been when he'd been doing his rotations in London. They'd been junior doctors at the same time, in fact.

'What a surprise!' he exclaimed, shaking David's hand. He kissed Sarah's cheek and grinned at her. 'I take it that you haven't kicked this reprobate into touch, then?'

'No. More fool me, eh?' Sarah laughed as she held up her hand so he could see the wedding band on her finger. 'We got married last year, so I doubt I'll be able to get rid of him now.'

'Congratulations,' Ryan said warmly, genuinely pleased for them. He looked round when he heard footsteps, smiling when Eve appeared round the side of the bus. 'Look who's here, Eve. David and Sarah—you remember them, don't you?'

'Of course,' Eve replied.

She shook hands with them but Ryan was very aware of how ill at ease she appeared. He frowned, wondering what was wrong. David and Sarah had been part of their set and they'd got on very well together.

However, he had the distinct impression that they were the last people Eve had wanted to see.

'I must say I'm surprised to see you here, Eve,' Sarah said curiously. 'The last I heard, you'd moved abroad. When did you get back?'

'About six months ago,' Eve replied quietly.

Ryan could hear the tension in her voice and felt more perplexed than ever. Something was definitely wrong, although he had no idea what.

'Really? So have you returned to medicine?' Sarah continued, obviously keen to find out more.

'Yes.'

'Oh, good. That's great.' Sarah sounded a bit surprised by the brevity of the answer. She glanced from Eve to Ryan. 'So how did you guys meet up? Did you keep in touch or something?'

'No. Eve accepted a post at Dalverston General when she decided to return to medicine,' Ryan explained. 'I've been working there for several years now and it was a real surprise when she turned up out of the blue, a pleasant one, mind you.'

Sarah laughed. 'I'm sure it was. You two were always the best of friends, weren't you? We all thought you'd make the perfect couple until Eve started seeing Damien.' She turned to Eve. 'Are you still in touch with him, by the way?'

'No. I haven't seen him in a long time.'

Ryan heard the panic in Eve's voice and all of a sudden realised what was wrong. She was scared stiff, terrified at the thought of her ex tracking her down. He cursed under his breath, calling himself every kind of a fool for not realising it sooner. Slamming the back doors, he put his hand under her elbow.

'It's been great seeing you guys again but I'm afraid we're going to have to go. Maybe we'll run into one another again some time.'

'You never know,' David replied easily. He turned to leave then glanced back. 'I'll tell Damien I saw you, shall I, Eve? He may want to get in touch.'

He didn't wait for a reply as he and Sarah hurried off to rejoin their friends. Ryan took one look at Eve's white face and knew that he needed to get her on the bus. She looked on the point of passing out and that was the last thing he wanted when it would invite all sorts of awkward questions.

'Come along.'

He steered her to the steps, keeping his hand under her elbow as he helped her on board. Fortunately the front seat was vacant so he sat her down and fastened her seat belt because she didn't appear capable of doing it herself. She just sat there, staring straight ahead, her face devoid of colour, and Ryan knew that he would never forgive himself if there was any come-back from what had happened.

What if Damien contacted her? If David told him where Eve was working, he might very well do so and the thought was more than he could bear. He may have raised a lot of money for Scott's fund in the past few days but it wouldn't mean a thing if he'd put Eve at risk!

They'd booked into a guest house on the outskirts of Betws y Coed. Eve got off the bus and followed the others inside. Despite their tiredness, everyone was in high spirits and she did her best to join in but it was impossible. She kept thinking about what would happen if Damien tracked her down. She was over him—she was sure about that. However, the thought of having to see him again made her feel sick.

'Let's get you sorted out.' Ryan rang the old-fashioned bell on the counter. As soon as the proprietor appeared, he introduced himself and asked for the key to his room. Eve had no time to protest as he led her up the stairs to the first floor. Unlocking the bedroom door, he ushered her inside. 'I'll fetch your bag up in a minute. I just need to make sure everyone's all right first.'

'Thank you.' Eve bit her lip when she felt tears sting her eyes. She hated feeling so afraid, hated the fact that Damien still had a hold over her. Until she could rid herself of this fear, she would never be free of him.

'Don't.' Ryan's voice was so gentle that the tears spilled over.

'I don't want to feel like this,' she murmured, choking back a sob. 'I hate it, hate the fact that he can make me feel so *scared*!'

'I know, sweetheart. I understand, really I do.' He gathered her into his arms and she felt the shudder that passed through him. 'You've just got to hold onto the thought that one day you'll be able to think about him and not feel anything.'

'Do you really believe it will happen?' she asked hollowly.

'Yes, I do.' He tilted her face so he could look into her eyes. 'You're strong and you're brave and one day this will all seem like a bad dream.' He smoothed his thumb over her trembling lips. 'It will get easier, Eve, I promise you. I'll make sure it does!'

Eve felt her breath catch when she saw the expression in his eyes, a mixture of tenderness and something else, something that made her heart race, although not from fear this time. She knew that he was going to kiss her and just for a moment panic rose inside her. And then his mouth found hers, warm and so achingly gentle that her panic melted away. This was Ryan and he would never hurt her. He would always protect her.

It was a moment Eve knew she would remember for the rest of her life. She had been living with fear for so long but there was nothing to fear any more. Ryan was here and he would make things right, support her, help her. And maybe—just maybe—she could help him too.

It was that final thought that unlocked the last of her reservations. Reaching up, she drew his head down so she could deepen the kiss. She felt him tense and then the next second he was kissing her with a hunger that couldn't be denied. Ryan needed this kiss as much as she did!

They were both breathing heavily when they broke apart. Eve could feel the blood pounding through her veins, filling her with life and warmth, and it was the most wonderful feeling after existing in a state of limbo for so long. Ryan rested his forehead against hers and she could feel him trembling.

'I didn't plan this, Eve. I want you to know that.'

'I do.' She took a shuddery breath. 'I didn't plan it either, just in case you thought I had.'

He laughed softly. 'So you don't have designs on me, then? I'm gutted.'

'Hmm, I doubt that.' Eve chuckled, loving the fact that he could tease her even at a moment of such high emotion. 'I imagine there have been enough women who've had designs on you to feed your ego.'

'One or two.' He drew back and his expression was solemn all of a sudden. 'But none of them meant anything to me, Eve. Not like you do.'

He broke off when there was a knock on the door. Eve smoothed back her hair as he went to answer it. What had he been about to say? That he cared for her? That he loved her?

Her heart leapt even though she knew it was too soon to think along those lines. She couldn't afford to get carried away by the heat of the moment. It had been a shock to see Sarah and David again and it was understandable if she got things out of proportion. Only she didn't honestly believe that was what had happened. Did she?

Her feelings for Ryan weren't governed by past events. He may have helped to unlock her emotions but how she felt right now wasn't a reaction to what she'd been through before. She bit her lip. Her feelings for Ryan were pure and unsullied by anything else.

CHAPTER ELEVEN

IT TOOK RYAN some time to sort out the problem with
their accommodation. It turned out that there weren't
enough rooms for them all even though he had booked
the correct number. By the time he dug out a copy of
the confirmation email he'd received, everyone was
starting to look really fed up.

He passed it over the desk so the proprietor could
read it. 'Here you are. As you can see from this, I
booked and paid for four rooms.'

'I don't know what's happened then, Dr Sullivan.'
Mr Jones shook his head. 'I've only got you down for
three rooms, I'm afraid, although it's obviously my
mistake. The problem is that I don't have another room
available. We're fully booked, you see.'

'In that case, can you suggest somewhere else?'
Ryan asked tersely. He didn't need this hassle, he really didn't. Not when he so desperately wanted to get
back to Eve.

He bit back a groan. That kiss may have been wonderful but he had been wrong to allow it to happen.
It could so easily have led to something more if they
hadn't been interrupted, and that was the last thing

he wanted. Once he made love to Eve he would never be able to stick to his decision; he would *have* to stay with her even though he knew he could ruin her life.

'I doubt you'll find another room in Betws y Coed at this time of the year,' Gwyn Jones said apologetically. 'What with it being Easter, you understand, everywhere will be fully booked. No, the only thing I can suggest is that you use the cabin. We don't normally let it this early in the year but it won't take me long to get it ready. I should warn you, though, that I usually rent it out to families so it's rather basic.'

'Fine. I'll take it.' Ryan didn't waste time debating the idea. He turned to the rest of the party and shrugged. 'Sorry about this, guys, but it can't be helped. I'll take the cabin so sort out which rooms you want.'

'Eve won't mind, will she?' Marie asked guilelessly. 'I mean, she might not fancy the idea of roughing it.'

'I'm sure she'll be fine about it,' Ryan said firmly, although he had no idea how Eve would feel. Maybe he should have consulted her, he mused as he ran back upstairs. Given her the choice. They could even have tried to swop everyone around so she could share with someone else, only that would have invited even more speculation, wouldn't it? He sighed as he reached the bedroom. He couldn't do right for doing wrong, it seemed.

Eve was sitting on the bed when he went in and he was relieved to see that she looked more composed than she had done earlier. 'All sorted?' she asked.

'Kind of.' He gave a little shrug, trying to play it cool, no mean feat in view of the fact that the moment he'd set eyes on her, his body had responded in time-honoured fashion. 'There's been a mix-up with our booking. They've only reserved three rooms for us instead of the four I booked. Mr Jones has offered us the use of his cabin to make up the shortfall and I've agreed as it's unlikely we'll find anywhere else. I'm not sure what it will be like, though. He described it as basic so say if you don't fancy staying there and I'll see if I can juggle everyone around.'

'I don't think that's possible, do you?' Eve demurred, standing up. 'Marie and Steve are the only ones who could feasibly swop places and it isn't fair to ask them when they've been looking forward to spending some time together.' She picked up her bag and shrugged. 'I'm sure it'll be fine.'

'Well, so long as you're happy to give it a go,' Ryan said, doubtfully.

'It isn't a problem—really.'

She gave him a quick smile as she headed out of the door. Ryan followed her down the stairs, wondering if he was imagining the fact that she seemed to be trying to set a little distance between them. He sighed as he waited for Mr Jones to fetch the keys to the cabin. Maybe Eve had decided, as he had done, that it would be foolish to get carried away by the heat of the moment. After all, she had as much to lose as him. She needed to concentrate all her efforts on getting her life back on track. She didn't have time to think about starting a relationship.

The cabin was much nicer than she had expected. Eve smiled as she looked around the simply furnished inte-

rior. The walls were of bare cedar, caulked and sealed
to keep out any draughts, making it feel very cosy.
Soft furnishings in various shades of green added to
the charm of the place plus there was a tiny kitchen
and a bathroom, as well as two bedrooms, the largest
built into the mezzanine level and offering a wonderful view of the woods. Turning to Ryan, she laughed
in delight.

'I'd say we've struck it lucky, wouldn't you? This
is lovely!'

'It is nice,' he agreed, looking around. 'It's so quiet
too because we're well away from the road back here.'

'It's perfect,' she assured him, and he laughed.

'Phew! That's a relief. I did wonder if I was being
a bit presumptuous by expecting you to rough it in
a cabin.'

'Oh, I think I can cope very happily with this.'

She smiled at him and felt her heart leap when he
smiled back. He'd seemed a little withdrawn since he'd
returned to tell her about the mix-up with the rooms
and it was a relief to know that he seemed to have
got over whatever had been troubling him. Maybe
he'd been having doubts about that kiss too but it had
happened and there was no point regretting it. It was
what happened from here on that mattered more and
she had no idea what that was going to be.

The thought was a little disquieting in view of the
fact that she wasn't sure what she wanted to do. Eve
pushed it to the back of her mind as she headed into
the kitchen. Opening the miniature-sized fridge, she
took out a fresh carton of milk. 'It looks like our host

has provided us with a few necessities. How about I make us some tea while you fetch the bags?'

'Good idea. I won't be long.'

Ryan sketched her a wave and left. Eve filled the kettle and set it to boil, opening cupboards at random until she found what she needed. She laid cups and saucers, milk jug and sugar bowl on a tray then made the tea. There was even a packet of ginger biscuits so she put some on a plate and had everything ready by the time he came back. He grinned as he took stock.

'Quite the little domestic goddess, aren't you?' he teased, leaving their bags by the door.

'I have my moments,' she retorted, carrying the tray into the living room and setting it down on a rustic-style coffee table next to the sofa. She poured the tea then offered him a biscuit. 'No scones, I'm afraid, so these will have to do.'

'Hmm, I may have to downgrade you from fully fledged goddess to trainee if you haven't baked any scones,' he said, grinning.

'Oh, dear!' Eve rolled her eyes. 'I'm not sure I can stand the thought of being marked down.'

'I'm sure you'll survive. You're a lot tougher than you look, Eve.'

'Do you think so?'

He must have heard the doubt in her voice. He put down his cup and looked steadily back at her. 'Yes, I do. You wouldn't have got to this point if you hadn't been tough and brave too.'

'I didn't feel very brave when we bumped into Sarah and David,' she admitted. 'I thought I was going to collapse into a quivering little heap of jelly.'

'Because you were scared at the thought of Damien tracking you down?' he said gently, and she sighed.

'Yes. Oh, I know it's silly but the thought of seeing him again makes me feel all churned up inside.'

'Because you still have feelings for him?'

'I suppose so.' She frowned, wondering how best to explain how she felt about her ex. She didn't want to burden Ryan with her problems after all. She looked up in surprise when he suddenly stood up.

'I'm sure you'll work it out, Eve. As I said, you're strong and you're brave and in the end you'll sort things out. Right, I'll take our bags through. Which room do you fancy? How about the mezzanine? You'll get a wonderful view from up there.'

'I…um… Thank you.'

Eve watched him walk over and pick up their bags. He didn't look at her as he carried her case up the open-tread staircase. He came back down and took his bag into the other bedroom, closing the door behind him, and she was more confused than ever. Had she said something to upset him?

She ran back over their conversation but couldn't work it out and sighed. She was imagining it, reading too much into everything that happened. The problem was that she was so aware of Ryan that every word was far too significant. She needed to get a little balance back into her life, start seeing the situation for what it was. Ryan was her friend and, despite that kiss, he had every intention of remaining her friend too.

Ryan stayed in his room until it became clear that he couldn't stay holed up in there any longer. Eve would start to wonder what was wrong if he continued to hide himself away. Did he really want to admit how hard it had hit him to discover that she still had feelings for her ex? No way!

He opened the door, fixing a smile to his mouth when he saw her sitting on the sofa reading a magazine. 'Enjoying a few minutes' peace and quiet?'

'Hmm. It has been rather hectic, hasn't it?' she replied coolly, so coolly that he felt slightly miffed.

Did she have to make it clear that their kiss had meant nothing to her?

'It has. Still, we achieved our objective even though it was touch and go at one point,' he replied evenly, not wanting her to suspect anything was amiss.

'You did wonders to meet the deadline after having to deal with that accident,' she said more warmly.

'The guys were great,' he agreed, feeling his heart lift. He sighed because all it took was the tiniest encouragement and his emotions were off and running again. It made him see just how deep he was in and how dangerous it would be to keep on spending time with her when they got back to Dalverston. If he was to protect her then he had to keep away from her, although maybe that wasn't as important as he'd believed if she was still in love with her ex.

The thought made him wince and not just because he hated the idea of her loving another man. He'd seen the statistics and knew that many victims of abuse returned to their abuser. He couldn't bear to think that Eve would make the same mistake. He swung round, knowing that he had to make her see sense.

'What are you going to do if Damien does get in

touch?' He frowned when she didn't answer. 'Come on, Eve. Surely you aren't crazy enough to get back with him?'

'Of course not!' She sounded so shocked that he grimaced.

'Sorry. It's just that… No, it doesn't matter.'

'Yes, it does. Why on earth would you think that I'd get involved with him again after what he did?'

'A lot of women do,' he said simply.

'Maybe. But I'm not one of them.' She hugged her arms around herself and he saw the tremor that ran through her. 'I don't want to see or speak to him ever again.'

'Because you're afraid that you won't be able to re-sist?' he said hollowly, his heart aching all the more.

'No, because the thought of being near him makes me feel sick.' Her voice wobbled. 'When I first made the break I went to stay at my parents' house in the Dordogne. I thought I'd be safe there, beyond his reach, but I was wrong. He managed to track me down and followed me.'

'What happened?' Ryan said roughly, feeling slightly sick himself.

'He tried to persuade me to go back to him, prom-ised that he would never do anything to hurt me ever again.' She shrugged. 'He sounded very convincing too until he spoiled it by getting angry when I refused.'

Ryan's hands clenched. 'Did he hit you?'

'No. I didn't give him the chance. Luckily enough, the gardener was working that day so I told Damien that I would tell him to call the police.' She smiled thinly. 'Damien couldn't leave fast enough after that.'

'Thank heavens!' Ryan exclaimed, shuddering at the thought of what might have happened. 'Was that the last you saw of him?'

'Oh, yes. I realised that I needed to put more distance between us so I went to Florida. One of my friends lives there and she'd just had twins and needed someone to look after them when she went back to work.' She smiled. 'I stayed there for the next couple of years, two very happy years, too. Looking after the girls helped me focus on what I wanted to do with my life, which was to return to medicine. Once the twins were old enough for pre-school, I came back to England and started applying for jobs. And finished up at Dalverston.'

'So if Damien does contact you, you're pretty sure that you'll give him short shrift?' Ryan said carefully, trying not to let her know how important her answer was to him.

'Absolutely sure.' She looked up and he saw the certainty in her eyes. 'I'm not in love with him any longer if, indeed, I was ever in love with him in the first place.'

'What do you mean?'

'That I've started to realise my feelings weren't all they seemed. Oh, I was very attracted to him in the beginning and I don't deny it. He was charming, sophisticated, witty—but now I can see that I was *flattered* by his attentions more than anything else. I don't think I was ever really in love with him if I'm honest.'

Eve could feel her heart pounding. Its beat was so loud that it drowned out every other sound. She saw

Ryan stand up, watched him take the couple of steps that were all that were needed to reach her, but she heard nothing apart from the beating of her own heart. When he held out his hand, she took it, feeling the strength of his fingers as they closed around hers. He helped her to her feet then just stood there, waiting...

Eve leant forward until her mouth met his. It was the merest touch of flesh on flesh but it was enough. She shuddered as a host of sensations shot through her. She felt both hot and cold, excited and scared, and wonderfully, vibrantly alive. It was as though she'd been asleep for the past few years, her life on hold, her emotions barely ticking over, until this moment. Although the kiss they'd shared before had started to unlock her feelings it was this whisper of a kiss that was the real key. This kiss that was so gentle, so giving, so totally fulfilling.

'Eve.'

Ryan's voice was as soft as a summer breeze and she shuddered again. She could hear the wonder it held and knew that he was equally affected by what was happening. She laid her hand flat on his chest, feeling the heavy beat of his heart beneath her palm. His heart was racing too because he felt the same as she did.

Raising herself up on tiptoe, she pressed her mouth to his and felt the shudder that passed through him. She could feel ripples of it spreading across his chest, feel its echo pass into her, and gloried in the fact that they were sharing this moment. Maybe it wouldn't last—couldn't last—but for now they were no longer two separate people but a couple. A pair. And what one felt, the other felt too.

The thought was just too much, too much to ignore, too much to deal with. Eve stepped back, knowing that Ryan could see every single emotion she was feeling. It would have scared her before to know she was so vulnerable but not now. Not with him. Ryan would never hurt her. He would always protect her.

'I want us to make love,' she told him, her voice barely above a whisper. 'I want us to make love so that I can feel like a real woman again. It's not just for my sake, though. I think it's what you want too, isn't it, Ryan?'

'Yes!'

The word seemed to explode from his lips, filled with so many emotions that Eve felt giddy as she tried to sort them out. However, in the end there was only one that mattered, only one she cared about. Ryan wanted her and that was enough.

She held out her hand and he took it, raised it to his lips and kissed her palm. He didn't say a word as she led him up the stairs but neither did she. They didn't need words, didn't need questions or answers when they both knew what they wanted. And what they wanted was to make love.

Eve let go of his hand when they reached the bed-room and unbuttoned her shirt. She shrugged it off and let it fall to the floor. A camisole came next, the soft whisper of cloth barely disturbing the silence as it too dropped onto the bare wooden floorboards. Her boots, socks and jeans followed until she was dressed only in her underwear, plain white cotton rather than seductive satin, not that it appeared Ryan needed to be seduced. Tossing back her hair, she looked at him, her desire growing when she saw the expression in his eyes. That he wanted her, desperately, wasn't in doubt.

'Your turn now,' she said huskily, moved almost beyond bearing.

He held her gaze as he slipped off his sweater and tossed it onto the pile of clothing. A T-shirt followed then boots, socks and jeans. Eve bit her lip as she took stock of his powerful figure. Everywhere she looked he was all hard muscle and sinew and it was such a stark contrast to her own body with its soft curves that she couldn't help being aware of the differences. When he took her hand and tugged her towards him, she resisted, overwhelmed by what was happening.

'Eve?'

This time her name was a question, one she had to answer too. Eve knew that if she told him she had changed her mind, he would accept it. But was that really what she wanted to do? Was she sorry she had started this? Did she want to stop?

Questions seemed to rush at her from all sides until she could no longer think and then Ryan spoke again, softly and with infinite tenderness. 'Whatever you decide is fine, Eve. I just want you to be happy.'

Her mind cleared and she knew what she wanted, which was Ryan holding her, loving her, making her see how good it could feel to be a woman. Gripping tight hold of his hand, she led him to the bed.

CHAPTER TWELVE

RYAN COULD FEEL every muscle in his body quivering as Eve led him to the bed. It felt as though every tiny bit of him was so tightly strung that he would shatter into hundreds of pieces. Making love had never felt like this before, never been so intense, so all-consuming, so…so *important*! But this was Eve and this was very different from anything that had gone before.

Anxiety overwhelmed him as he watched her sit down on the bed. He sank to his knees in front of her, taking her face between his hands. Maybe she didn't need reassuring but he did! He wanted to erase any bad memories she might be harbouring and he wasn't sure if he could do that, if he was skilled enough as a lover. What he had learned in the past might not be enough and the thought filled him with dread. He would never forgive himself if Eve hated their love-making, hated his touch.

'Don't.' Her voice was low but strangely firm. Ryan drew back and looked at her. 'You're worried about what's going to happen and if it will bring back a lot of awful memories, aren't you?'

'Yes,' he said simply, because he wouldn't lie. 'I

couldn't bear to think that I might scare you, sweet-heart.'

'You won't.' She leant forward and kissed him lightly on the mouth and her eyes were clear and un-afraid when she looked at him. 'You're not him, Ryan. You're you. And I trust you.'

Relief poured through him as he gathered her to him and held her close. All of a sudden his confidence came roaring back and he knew it was going to be all right, that he had nothing to fear. Making love with Eve was going to be perfect. For her. For him. For both of them.

He groaned as he let his hand slide down her back, feeling her skin glide beneath his palm like the finest silk. And like the finest silk it started out by feeling cool to the touch but it soon warmed up. He let his fingers splay against her back, warming her skin be-fore its heat seeped back into him like the most sen-sual form of osmosis.

Even now, they were sharing their feelings, he re-alised in wonderment. It had never been like this be-fore. Although passion may have come quickly there'd never been this closeness, this intensity. It was only with Eve that he felt this way; only with her that he would experience this magic.

Tears burned his eyes as he bent and kissed her, letting his mouth say all the things he couldn't say with his voice. He loved her so much but he daren't tell her that. He had to remember that he could hurt her and that was the one thing he would never do. For all these years he had avoided commitment and now it was the thing he longed for most of all. He wanted

Eve from now to eternity but he couldn't have her. They could only ever have this one night and although it wasn't enough, he intended to make it special. One precious night to see him through all the empty years that lay ahead.

Eve closed her eyes as she savoured the feel of Ryan's mouth as he scattered kisses across her face. Everywhere his lips touched, they left behind a tiny pulse point of heat, a gentle brand that proclaimed her as his, and she shivered. The thought of being branded this way would have terrified her at one time but not now. Not when it was Ryan marking her as his.

His lips found hers again and she sighed, loving the fact that kissing him felt so right, so natural. She'd learned to fake her response in the past, afraid of letting Damien know how much she had loathed his touch, but there was no need for that now. There was nothing false about this passion she felt: it was one hundred per cent real. She could feel it deep inside, feel it building second by second until her whole body throbbed with it. What she felt for Ryan was real, magical and mind-blowing, but real.

Wrapping her arms around his neck, she urged him closer, shuddering when she felt the weight of his body settle over hers. She was still wearing her underclothes and the softly abrasive rasp of cotton on her nipples made her shiver with longing. She could feel them peak, feel them tauten into tight little buds that begged to be noticed, and they got their wish. When Ryan lowered his head and drew her nipple into his mouth, she cried out, unable to hold back the rush of sensations that poured through her.

'Are you all right?' He drew back to look at her and what he saw obviously reassured him. 'You don't need to answer that,' he murmured seductively.

Eve took him at his word and didn't bother, couldn't have done so anyway because his mouth had found her other nipple and was lavishing the same attention on it too. Her hands clenched as wave after wave of sensation poured through her, flurries of heat that found their way to the very core of her femininity. When he slid his hand down her body and cupped her, she jerked violently.

His fingers splayed across the plain white cotton pants, one finger lightly, tantalisingly caressing her, and Eve shuddered. She couldn't recall ever feeling so aroused before, knew it hadn't happened. It was only Ryan's touch that could arouse her this way, only Ryan who could show her how good it really felt to be a woman. No matter what happened in the future, she would treasure this moment and be glad that it had happened.

The thought trickled coldly through the heat but there was no time to dwell on it, definitely no time to allow it to spoil the magic. Ryan slid her panties off her hips and tossed them aside then removed the final item of his clothing. Eve gasped when she saw the strength and power of his erection, saw how much he wanted her, a reaction that wasn't lost on him either.

She bit her lip as she watched him reach down and take a condom from his wallet. He slid it on then took her face between his hands and looked deep into her eyes. 'It's not too late to stop, Eve. If this isn't what you want then say so.'

His concern was just too much. Eve's eyes swam with tears as she laid her hand against his cheek. 'Thank you.'

'What for?' He kissed her softly, his eyes filled with tenderness.

'For giving me a choice,' she whispered. 'Even though I don't need to choose...'

She barely had a chance to finish what she was saying before his mouth found hers again. Eve closed her eyes, savouring the taste of his tongue as it slid between her lips in the moment before he entered her. Her body opened to him at once, drawing him in, welcoming him, and she felt him shudder. Had he been afraid she wouldn't want him when the time came? she wondered tenderly, then wondered no more because it was impossible to think about anything except what was happening.

Heat and light filled her, a glow that seemed to start somewhere deep inside her and spread with every powerful thrust of his body. By the time it had consumed her totally, she couldn't think, couldn't breathe, couldn't do anything except let Ryan carry her away to a place she had never been before. As she tumbled over the edge into oblivion, she knew that what had happened had transformed her life and that she would never be the same again. She was someone different now that Ryan had made love to her.

Consciousness returned slowly, the heavy pounding of his heart gradually slowing to a less frantic pace. Ryan lay on his back, his eyes closed but his other senses working overtime. He could hear the steady beat of Eve's heart as she lay beside him and marvelled at the fact that he had never been aware of anyone's heart beating before. But this was Eve. This was different. This was love.

A wave of unbearable sadness rose up inside him and he opened his eyes, afraid that he wouldn't be able to contain it if he lay there and thought things like that. He'd known from the start that, no matter what happened, no matter how wonderful it felt to make love to Eve, it couldn't lead anywhere. Now he had to make sure that she understood it too.

'Are you all right?' he asked quietly, wondering dully how to set about it. It was the hardest thing he'd ever had to do and he was suddenly afraid that he would make a mess of it. He couldn't bear to think that he might *hurt* her when he was trying so desperately to protect her.

'Fine.' She turned and smiled at him, and Ryan felt his heart turn to lead when he saw the joy in her eyes. It was obvious what she thought and it was all his fault. He should have set out the ground rules in advance, made sure she'd understood where this was going, which was nowhere.

'You're doing it again, Ryan.'

Her voice broke into his thoughts and he frowned. 'What do you mean?'

'That you're worrying in case, well, in case I read too much into what's happened.'

She gave a little shrug and he blinked in surprise. Was she right? Was he misreading the signals, attributing far more meaning to what they'd done than she was? Part of him didn't want to believe it while another, more cowardly part hoped it was true.

'I don't want to hurt you, Eve. You've been through enough,' he began, then stopped. He couldn't lie, wouldn't even try. He had to tell her the truth even if he couldn't tell her it all. 'What I'm trying to say is that I care about you, Eve. A lot.'

He took her hand, held it lightly in his, afraid that if he held it any tighter he would crush her fingers. His emotions had never felt so charged, so raw. It would take very little to let it all pour out—his love for her, how he ached to be part of her future and for her to be part of his, and that was what he couldn't do. He must never let Eve persuade him he was wrong; he couldn't take that risk.

'I know you do.' She turned her hand over, gripping his hard, and his resolve wavered. It was all he could do not to pull her into his arms, tell her how he really felt, and allow himself to be convinced. They could have it all if he did—love, marriage, the happily-ever-after—everything couples dreamt about...

Except children.

'I care about you too, Ryan. But we both know the time isn't right, don't we?' She sighed as she smoothed the pad of her thumb over his palm. 'If this had happened a few months down the line then maybe we could have worked something out but it's too soon. Or it is for me anyway.'

'Because of what happened to you?' he said gruffly, hating the fact that she was handing him a get-out-of-jail-free card even though he needed it so desperately.

However, the thought that she was still affected by her past experiences was hard to swallow.

'Indirectly.' She frowned. 'It sounds crazy but it's not what I went through with Damien that's worrying me most. It's the fact that I still need to find *myself.* I had so many plans, you see, so many things I wanted to achieve. We used to talk about what we intended to do when we were training, didn't we, and I've realised that I still want all of that.

'I want a career I love and I want to get married and have a family one day too. I want it all back, everything I dreamt about, everything I lost.' She sighed. 'I don't think I can do that if I'm trying to build a relationship. I honestly don't think I'm strong enough.'

He could understand her reasoning, understand and agree with it, but it still hurt to know that he came second to her plans, that her feelings for him weren't as strong as his were for her. Ryan shook his head to clear it of such selfish ideas. After all, he was doing the same thing, wasn't he? He was applying reason to his emotions, working out what was best for her, for him, for both of them.

'If that's what you want, Eve, then it's fine,' he told her, although the words almost choked him.

'You do understand, don't you?' She looked anxiously into his eyes. 'It's not that I don't care about you, Ryan. I do. An awful lot. It would be only too easy to let whatever happened simply happen. But in here...' she touched her heart '...I know that I'll regret it. I need to find myself before I have anything to offer you.'

'I understand, sweetheart. Really I do.' He bent and kissed her on the lips then stood up. If he didn't leave right now, he wouldn't be able to keep up the pretence. He would have to tell her how he really felt, that she was making a mistake, that he loved her and that he would help make all her dreams come true.

All except one very important one. If Eve stayed with him she would never become a mother.

The thought tore his heart to shreds, ripped it apart and tossed it aside in a bloodied little heap. Ryan's legs were trembling as he made for the stairs. Hard though it was, he could accept that he would never be a father. What he couldn't accept was that Eve would never be a mother.

'I think we both need a bit of breathing space,' he told her roughly. 'Why don't you have a rest? We're meeting the others for dinner at seven so there's plenty of time.'

'I shall.' His foot found the first tread when she continued and he paused reluctantly. 'What just happened, Ryan…well, it was magical.'

'For me too,' he said gruffly, and ran down the stairs. The floorboards felt cold beneath his feet, cold and hard like the lump in his throat. Going into the bedroom, he closed the door and made himself breathe in and out just to prove that he was capable of breathing, capable of living. Oh, he knew he was, knew that he would manage it somehow. He didn't have a choice. He had to live his life the best way he could but it would always be a second-best existence without Eve there to share it with him.

They arrived back in Dalverston at lunchtime on Monday. Eve was first to be dropped off and she smiled broadly as she waved goodbye, hoping no one could tell how desperately sad she felt. As she watched the minibus drive away, she had to stop herself running after it, stop herself running after Ryan. She had done the right thing—she had! She just needed to convince herself now.

She let herself into the flat, leaving her bag by the door because it was too much effort to unpack it. The place felt so cold and quiet and she shivered. She'd grown used to having people around and had enjoyed the company but it was one person she missed most, one person she would continue to miss for however long it took her to get over what had happened. Would she succeed or would she always wonder if she'd made a mistake? The thought filled her with dread. She didn't want to face the future filled with doubts.

She went into the kitchen and made some tea then sat at the table, letting it go cold. She hadn't planned to tell Ryan what she had: it had just slipped out. Maybe it was the fact that she'd sensed he'd had doubts that had triggered her own misgivings, but she'd realised it would be a mistake to rush into something they could regret. Maybe she *did* love him but until she was a whole person again she couldn't make any sort of commitment. It wouldn't be fair to short-change him, to expect him to love her the way she was. They needed to be on an equal footing, both sure of who they were. Their relationship wouldn't work if Ryan was having to act as her prop.

Eve poured the tea down the drain and took her case into the bedroom. She had to start as she intended to go on and that meant taking charge of her life, even the insignificant bits like unpacking. She'd lost too many years drifting along and she refused to lose any more. And if she made a success of it, well, who knew what might happen?

Hope shone brightly inside her. Maybe, just maybe, once she had found herself, she and Ryan could try again.

If he wanted to.

If he was willing.

If he loved her.

Ryan was on early on Tuesday morning and arrived at the hospital shortly before six a.m. Marie was in the staffroom when he went in and she grinned at him.

'So how are the legs? Mine are as stiff as boards.'

'Mine too,' he agreed, shoving his jacket in the locker. 'I didn't know that muscles could ache as much as this.'

'Good,' Marie declared with a sad lack of sympathy. 'I'd hate to be the only one suffering!'

'You're not,' he assured her. 'Still, it was a brilliant effort, wouldn't you say?'

'It was, especially after us having to stop to help with that RTA.' Marie closed her locker door. 'Did the Scottish police get back to you, by the way?'

'Yes, they did. The father and the two kids were discharged but the two women are still in ICU,' he began, then stopped when the door opened and Eve appeared.

'Morning.'

She smiled at them as she went over to her locker and Ryan did his best to smile back but it was too damned hard. How could he pretend that he was fine when his heart was broken? He'd spent the most miserable night of his entire life, spent it thinking about Eve and everything that had happened—and everything that could never happen too. Oh, he had tried to see sense, tried to see it from her side as well as his, but it hadn't helped. It couldn't do, not when it all came down to one simple yet painful fact: he and Eve couldn't be together. Not now. Not ever.

'Right, I'll go and see what's been happening in our absence.' He swung round, terrified that he would do the unforgivable and say something he shouldn't. He and Eve couldn't share their lives, couldn't be a couple. *He* knew that but his foolish heart didn't. If he listened to what it was saying then he would never do what he had to do, what was right.

He went through to the unit and busied himself catching up. George Porter, the child with meningitis, was much better and was being discharged that day, which was excellent news. Most of the other children were on the mend too, although there'd been two admissions over the weekend who definitely needed his full attention. Whilst he would never wish any child to suffer, he was glad to have to focus on their needs. At least while he was concentrating on them, he wasn't thinking about himself and that had to be a bonus.

He sighed as he picked up the first child's file. That was the theory anyway. Whether it would work in practice remained to be seen.

CHAPTER THIRTEEN

'CAN YOU EXPLAIN again how Charlie came to sustain these injuries, Mrs Lawrence?'

Eve frowned when she heard the edge in Ryan's voice. It was obvious that there was something troubling him, although she wasn't sure what. She glanced at six-year-old Charlie Lawrence's admission notes, wondering if she would find a clue in there. The little boy had been brought into A and E the previous evening. The doctor who had examined him had sent him for an X-ray, which had revealed a badly fractured left femur. Charlie had been taken straight to Theatre where Ray McNulty, the paediatric orthopaedic surgeon, had reduced the fracture. So far, so routine. So why was Ryan digging deeper into this case?

'We already explained what happened,' Brian Lawrence put in before his wife could answer. 'It's all there in the notes, Doctor.'

'I know.' Ryan's smile was bland. It definitely didn't match the look in his eyes as he fixed the other man with a piercing stare. 'However, facts can tend to get a little, well, *distorted* when they're written down, so bear with me.' He turned to Amy Lawrence, his voice softening as he prompted her to answer. 'You were in the house on your own when Charlie fell down the stairs, is that correct, Mrs Lawrence?'

'I…ehem… Yes, that's right.'

Amy Lawrence glanced at her husband and Eve frowned when she realised how nervous the woman looked. She had the distinct impression that Mrs Lawrence was worried in case she said something wrong and her heart sank as she realised what was going on. Ryan obviously didn't believe that Charlie's leg had been broken by accident.

'I'd gone out for a drink with some friends.' Once again Brian Lawrence interrupted them. He turned to Eve and smiled winningly. 'Typical, isn't it? The one night I go out and something like this has to happen!'

He ruffled Charlie's hair. Eve's hands clenched when she saw the little boy flinch. That his father had noticed it too was obvious. Brian Lawrence gave his son a supposedly playful cuff around the ear. 'Remember what I'm always telling you, son. Don't play on the stairs or you could get hurt.'

Eve opened her mouth, unable to stand there and watch while he terrorised the child. Had he done this to Charlie, knocked him down the stairs in a fit of temper and fractured his leg? It was starting to look more and more likely.

'Mr Lawrence—' she began.

'Can you go to the office and phone Mr MacNulty, Dr Pascoe?' Ryan interrupted curtly, cutting her off. 'I need to double-check there were no complications during the operation. It could affect the length of time we have to keep Charlie in.'

Eve nodded, knowing that he'd been right to step in. If she accused Brian Lawrence of hurting the child without any evidence to back up the charge, it could have disastrous consequences. She went to the office and made the call. Ray was in Theatre but his secretary promised to ask him to phone back as soon as he was free. She'd just hung up when Ryan appeared, looking very grim.

'I came this close to decking him!' He held his finger and thumb a scant half-inch apart.

Eve sighed. 'You think the father's responsible for Charlie's injuries?'

'Yes. Did you see how the poor kid flinched when he touched him?'

'Yes. I didn't realise what was going on until then,' she admitted. 'Why did you suspect Charlie's injuries weren't accidental, though?'

'Because I checked his records and this is the third time he's been brought into hospital since Christmas.'

'Really?' She frowned. 'I didn't notice anything in his notes to that effect. Why didn't A and E flag it up?'

'That's something I intend to find out.' His tone was grim. 'If the poor kid's slipped through the net, how many others have done so as well?'

Eve shivered. The situation was a little too close to home for comfort. Ryan must have noticed her reaction and sighed.

'I know this is going to be really hard for you, Eve, so say if you'd rather not get involved.'

'Of course I want to be involved,' she countered.

'I can't just pretend that things like this don't happen. I need to deal with this kind of situation otherwise I won't be able to do my job properly.'

'I understand all that but it is rather different for you,' he pointed out.

'The fact that I've had first-hand experience of abuse gives me an edge.' She shrugged. 'I may be able to help Charlie's mother if she's being abused as well.'

'Are you sure you're up to it?' He frowned. 'I don't want you pushing yourself too hard. You're still getting over what happened to you, don't forget.'

'I'll back off if I feel it's too much for me,' she assured him, touched that he should try to protect her this way.

Marie poked her head round the door just then so they didn't say anything more. However, as she listened while Ryan explained his concerns to the ward sister, Eve couldn't help feeling more upbeat than she'd done since she'd come home. Ryan cared about her; he *really* cared. And she'd be lying if she claimed that it didn't make a difference to know how he felt. Maybe she had been a bit too hasty, telling him that she didn't have time for a relationship, she mused as she went back to the unit. After all, it would help enormously if he was at her side while she put her life back together. Knowing that Ryan was waiting for her would be the biggest incentive of all, but was it what he wanted?

He had always been commitment-phobic and nothing had happened to make her think he had changed. If he had done then surely he would have tried harder to persuade her to give him a chance? She sighed as she thought back to what had gone on at the weekend. Ryan might care about her. He might even love her in his own way but it obviously wasn't enough to make him reconsider his decision to remain single. Maybe he would change his mind one day when he met the right woman. However, it was clear that *she* wasn't that woman.

The day raced past. Between the normal business of dealing with his patients as well as trying to sort out the Charlie Lawrence situation, Ryan found himself working at full tilt. He was glad too. If his mind was fully occupied then it had less chance to wander along paths it shouldn't take. Eve was a friend. She could only ever be a friend. The familiar litany kept repeating itself over and over again but he still found it impossible to accept it as gospel.

The trouble was that he didn't want to accept it, didn't want to believe what he knew to be true, that Eve could never be his. It was too hard, too painful, too *everything* to erase her from his life this way. He had a feeling that he would never recover from it and it was a prospect that filled him with dread. An Eve-free future wasn't something he was looking forward to.

He went home after his shift, feeling very deflated. Although he was normally a positive person, there seemed very little light on his personal horizon. He made himself a sandwich then took it and a stack of journals into the sitting room. His to-be-read pile was almost as high as Ben Nevis and he needed to catch up with any new developments in the paediatric field. He was going to start applying for a consultant's post soon. If he couldn't have a wife and a family, at least he could have a career!

He was halfway through the first article when the doorbell rang. Ryan sighed as he got up. No doubt it would be someone trying to sell him something he didn't want. He flung open the front door and stopped dead, staring in surprise at Eve.

'What are you doing here?' he demanded with a sad lack of grace. However, in his defence the one person he had never expected to find on his doorstep was Eve.

'I wanted to return your mother's clothes.' Twin spots of colour appeared on her cheeks as she held out a bulging carrier bag and Ryan could have bitten off his tongue. Talk about how *not* to make someone feel welcome! 'Can you thank her for me and tell her that I've washed everything I used?'

She thrust the bag into his hands and turned to leave but there was no way that he was prepared to let her go without an apology. He hurried after her, catching hold of her arm to bring her to a halt.

'I'm sorry. I realise that wasn't the most welcoming of greetings but you caught me on the hop.' Unconsciously, his voice dropped because the feel of her flesh beneath his fingers was already having an effect. 'Won't you come in, Eve? Please.'

'I only came to return the clothes,' she said hoarsely, and he shuddered when he heard the raw emotion in her voice. She might be trying her best not to show how she felt but he could tell how difficult it was for her too. Eve may have decided that she needed time to put her life back together but it didn't mean that she didn't care about him.

The thought filled him with warmth, with light, with joy, and his fingers tightened around her arm. Even though he knew they couldn't be together, he still rejoiced at the thought. It took every scrap of willpower he could muster not to leap up and punch the air, in fact.

'I know. But there's no reason why you can't come in and have a cup of tea, is there?' He smiled persuasively, seeing the hesitancy in her eyes, and rejoiced once more even though he knew it was selfish. However, to know that she was tempted by his invitation was a definite boost to his ego.

'Well, if you're sure I'm not disturbing you?'

'You aren't.' He put his hands on her shoulders and turned her round. 'To be honest, you'll be doing me a favour.'

'How come?' she demanded as he steered her back up the path.

'Because I need an excuse not to have to read through all those dry-as-dust articles in the medical journals.' He slammed the door behind them and grinned at her. 'Oh, I know what you're thinking, that I should find them absorbing, but between you and me most of the guys who publish a paper can't write for toffee. They definitely wouldn't make it to the bestseller lists!'

She burst out laughing. 'How very unprofessional of you, Dr Sullivan. Tut, tut, I'm dismayed by your attitude.'

'Me too,' he said airily, leading the way to the kitchen. He switched on the kettle and laughed. 'I'm dismayed myself, especially as I need to be ahead of the game when I start applying for a consultant's post. But—hey!—what can I say?' He spread his hands wide. 'I can only assume that I must be a shallow sort of person because most of the articles I read bore me stiff.'

'Anyone less shallow is hard to imagine,' she said firmly.

'Thank you. I may ask you for a reference when I start applying for jobs.'

Ryan managed to hold his smile but it touched him to hear her say that and in that tone too. He was right, she *did* care, and the thought was the last one he needed in the circumstances. He busied himself making tea because it helped to do something practical. It was when he started thinking that the real problems began and he couldn't allow his thoughts to run away with him. Eve had brought back his mum's clothes. She hadn't come specifically to see him…

Had she?

He groaned as he dropped teabags into the mugs. Off they went, as fast as they could, racing like crazy. Had Eve come to return the clothes or had she another reason for visiting him? After all, she could have given the clothes to him at work and saved herself a journey. That seemed to suggest there was another reason for her visit but what? Had she changed her mind? Was she going to tell him that she'd been wrong and wanted them to be together? And if she did, what was *he* going to say? Would he stick to his guns or would temptation prove too much?

Questions, questions! One led to another and then to a third. His head was reeling as he tried to sort them out. What should he do? The right thing or the wrong? He knew what he wanted to do but the cost was too high. If he had Eve, *she* would never have a family. The fact that he couldn't have one either was immaterial at this point. It was Eve who mattered most, her needs which he had to focus on. She would never have a child if she stayed with him. Was that what he wanted? For her to have to give up one of her cherished dreams because of him?

'Ryan.'

He jumped when she said his name. Turning, he tried to smooth his face into a suitable expression, one that betrayed nothing of the sadness he felt. His thoughts had stopped running now and were sitting inside his head like cold lumps of lead. He couldn't do that to her. He couldn't take away something so precious. He couldn't do it for any reason and especially not so that he could have what he wanted which was her for all eternity.

'What's going on, Ryan?'

Her voice was low but he heard the steel in it and knew there was no point trying to lie his way out of it. He had to tell her the truth, every bit of it. And once that was done, he had to stand firm.

If he could.

Eve felt the blood rush to her head as Ryan went over to the table and sat down. It didn't need a genius to work out that whatever he was going to tell her, it wasn't good news. She clamped her lips tightly together as she went and sat down as well, afraid that she would tell him that she didn't want to hear it. She had to listen to what he had to say even if it wasn't what she wanted to hear.

She waited for him to begin, wishing that she had never started this. She could have returned his mother's clothes at work instead of coming here, but she'd convinced herself that it was only polite to give them back as soon as possible. It had been an excuse, of course. Not a very good one but the best she could come up with. It had been easier to tell herself that than admit that she'd wanted to see him. Maybe she *had* decided that she needed to put her life in order but that had been then. The moment she'd seen him today, she'd realised it wasn't possible to do it on her own. Ryan was part of her life now and she needed him around, needed him. Now she had to convince him that he needed her just as much.

If he did.

A shiver ran through her but Eve ignored it. She had to clear her mind of everything else, all the doubts, all the uncertainties, even the hope. She had to listen to what Ryan had to say without emotions getting in the way.

'Tell me what's going on, Ryan. I know something is wrong and I need to know what it is.'

He looked down at his hands for a moment then lifted his eyes to hers and she could have wept when she saw how bleak he looked. It took all her courage not to tell him to stop if it was going to hurt him this much, but she knew that she couldn't do that. He had to tell her. She had to listen. Neither of them had a choice.

'I told you that my brother died of long QT syndrome.' His voice was flat, emotionless, yet she jumped. It was the last thing she'd expected him to say.

'Yes,' she said quietly, trying to understand how that tragedy could impact on them.

Her breath caught as she realised what he might be saying. It was hard to keep the tremor out of her voice but it wasn't fair to expect him to cope with her emotions when he had to deal with his own. 'You also said that you aren't affected by LQTS.'

'That's right. I'm not.'

Once again he stared down at his hands and Eve felt her stomach quiver with nerves. They had reached the real crux of the issue and she was afraid that she wouldn't be able to handle what he had to tell her. But Ryan needed her to be strong. He needed her support. He needed her to be everything she'd been in the past, everything she was afraid she wasn't any more.

He suddenly looked up and Eve forced down the panic that had assailed her. 'I'm not affected by LQTS but I am a carrier of the gene that can cause it.'

He took a deep breath and she could see that his hands were trembling. Reaching out, she covered them with her own, wanting to comfort him any way she could. She loved him so much and that had to count for something, surely.

'It means that I could pass it on to my own children.' He turned his hands over and gripped hers, hard. 'That's why I can never have a family of my own, Eve. I can't take the risk of any child of mine inheriting such a cruel illness. It's also why I shall never get married. I wouldn't expect any woman to marry me knowing that we can never have children. It wouldn't be right and it wouldn't be fair. Especially not to you.'

CHAPTER FOURTEEN

EVE SAT QUITE still. She could hear the steady tick of the clock on the wall counting out the minutes, but it felt as though time had stopped. Ryan could never be a father. He would never have a child to love and care for. Of all the awful things that could have happened to him, this had to be the worst.

Tears streamed down her face but she barely noticed them. Her heart was aching, aching for him, aching for herself too. She had always wanted a family and had looked forward to the time when she would become a mother. Even in her darkest moments that dream had never deserted her. It had shone brightly, given her hope, encouraged her to look towards the future, a future that one day would be filled with love and laughter. Now she could feel it crumbling around the edges, flaking away, turning to dust. If Ryan couldn't have children then she could never have them either.

'Don't. Please don't cry, sweetheart. I can't bear it.'

His voice echoed with pain and Eve knew that she had to pull herself together. It was hard enough for him to know that he couldn't have something so important, without her making it worse. Standing up, she tore off a wad of kitchen roll and dried her eyes. Ryan didn't say anything as she came back and sat down. He seemed resigned to the fact that now he had told her the truth that was it. But was it? Was it the end for them? Or was there a way to work around this problem?

A glimmer of hope started to shimmer on the horizon, just the faintest glow but it was enough to be going on with. Eve blew her nose and looked directly at him. 'I don't know enough about this to speak with authority but are you sure there isn't anything you can do?'

'You mean like testing a foetus to see if it's inherited LQTS?' He shrugged. 'I can't give you a definitive answer. But even if I could, that isn't the point. I wouldn't expect any woman to have to go through the heartache of possibly having to abort a child because it's inherited this condition.'

Eve understood how he felt. The thought of terminating a pregnancy filled her with horror too. However, there had to be another way, surely? 'What about in vitro testing? That way only a foetus that proved to be clear of the gene would be implanted.'

'Even if it's possible—and I have no idea if it is because I've never gone into it—you know as well as I do that IVF is never an easy option. Apart from all the drugs that a woman would need to take to stimulate egg production, there'd be the stress of waiting to see if they'd produced a suitable foetus.' He shook his head. 'I wouldn't put any woman through that, Eve, especially when she could have got pregnant without all that hassle.'

'Nobody knows if they can get pregnant until they try,' she pointed out, praying that reason would help to convince him.

'No. But there's no reason to believe that *you* can't get pregnant, is there?' He cupped her cheek and his eyes were filled with an unbearable sadness. 'I couldn't do that to you, my darling. I couldn't put you through all that heartache and possible despair.'

'But surely it's up to me? It would be my decision, Ryan. I'd be going into it with my eyes open.'

'And that's what makes it worse.' His voice caught. 'Knowing that you love me enough to contemplate making such a huge sacrifice only makes me more determined to do what's right. I love you, Eve. And if circumstances were different I'd ask you to marry me like a shot. But they aren't different, are they? If we stay together then we can't have a family, *you* can never have a child. And that's not fair, is it?'

He stood up, making it clear that he'd said all he intended to say on the subject. Eve rose to her feet, her legs shaking as she made her way to the door and let herself out. Ryan didn't follow her and she didn't expect him to either. He could no more have stood at the door, waving her off, than she could have left him there and walked away.

She bit her lip as a sob rose to her throat. Of all the terrible things that had happened in her life this had to be the worst. She had lost the man she loved and there was no hope of getting him back.

The week passed, although most days Ryan felt as though he was merely treading water. He seemed to be stuck in that awful moment when he had told Eve why they could never be together. The scene constantly replayed itself inside his head, each word she'd uttered, everything he'd said. He tried to break the cycle, tried to bury it in some dark corner of his mind, but it refused to go quietly. Eve had been willing to take a chance and he'd refused. But what if he agreed? What if there was a way round this problem, as she'd suggested?

And what if they tried for a baby and it ended in heartache? How would she feel then? Would she be able to handle the disappointment? Would she still love him after he'd caused her such grief?

The questions were never-ending but the answer was always the same: he had to let her go. The only respite he got was when he was working. Focusing on his patients' needs quietened the internal voice so he spent more and more time at work. He saw Eve, of course. It was impossible not to and it was ever more stressful to watch her growing more withdrawn by the day.

Even Marie noticed it and said as much but he merely shrugged. How could he tell Marie that *he* was responsible for Eve slipping back into her shell? He'd wanted to help her and all he'd done was set her back to where she'd been. It was yet another thing to feel guilty about, to regret.

Social services had taken up the case of little Charlie Lawrence. Ryan gave instructions that Mr and Mrs Lawrence were to be supervised when they came to visit him. He'd decided to keep the boy in while the social workers investigated and only hoped they would be able to find out what had been going on before he had to discharge him. Although he was stretching the point by keeping Charlie in when he was fit enough to leave, Ryan had few qualms about it. The child needed protecting and that was more important than anything else.

Friday rolled around and he was relieved to discover that Eve was working late that day. She wasn't due in till six, which meant he wouldn't need to see her if he left on time. He was ready to depart on the dot of five, a fact that wasn't lost on Marie. She raised her brows when she found him in the staffroom, putting on his jacket.

'Hmm, you must have a hot date tonight if you're leaving on time.'

'How did you guess?' Ryan cracked a smile. The only date he wanted, hot or otherwise, was with Eve but that wasn't going to happen. Bending down, he searched for his car keys, which had fallen out of his pocket and slithered under the locker.

'So who's the lucky woman?' Marie continued. 'Anyone I know?'

'Nope. And I'm not going to tell you who she is either. Suffice it to say that hot doesn't do her justice!'

He straightened up and found himself staring at Eve. That she had heard what he'd said was obvious from her expression. Ryan's heart sank as she stalked past him and opened her locker. He couldn't believe she'd overheard that crass comment but what could he do? He could hardly explain that he'd been lying with Marie there, listening.

By the time he'd debated, Eve had hung up her

coat and was on her way out. He hurried after her but
she'd already entered the unit. He paused, not wanting
to follow her and cause a scene. Anyway, what was
the point? He and Eve weren't an item. They never
could be an item. Maybe it would be better to let her
think that he had moved on. He sighed as he made
for the lift. Better for her possibly but definitely not
better for him.

Eve couldn't believe how painful it was to discover
that Ryan was dating again. As she read through their
newest admission's notes, it was hard not to bawl her
eyes out. He'd claimed that he loved her but obviously his idea of love was a world away from hers!
Her breath hitched painfully on a sob and Tamsin,
who was setting up a drip, looked at her in concern.

'You OK, Eve?'

'Fine thanks.' Eve dredged up a smile. 'I bolted
down a sandwich before I came out and I think I may
have indigestion.'

'Oh, poor you!' the nurse exclaimed. 'I've some
peppermints in my locker. I'll get them for you when
I've finished this.'

'Thanks.' Eve smiled her thanks and moved away
from the bed. She went into the office and checked
the roster to see who was working that night. Penny
was on as well as Tamsin so they had sufficient cover
for once.

She went back to the unit and made her way round
the beds, talking to the children in turn. Although
nothing had been flagged up as needing her urgent
attention, she liked to be prepared so she could cover

every eventuality. She sighed because she certainly hadn't foreseen that Ryan would start dating again.

She came to Charlie Lawrence's bed last of all. They had moved him closer to the nurses' station so they could keep an eye on him. Eve smiled at him. He was such a sweet child and she had grown fond of him. 'So how are you tonight, Charlie?'

'Great,' he told her, smiling shyly back. 'Marie gave me this games console to play on. It's really cool!'

He showed Eve the console and explained the rules of the game he was playing. At his insistence, she had a go but didn't manage to score a single point. She shook her head as she handed it back to him.

'I'm rubbish, aren't I?'

'You just need to practise,' he assured her. His fingers whizzed over the buttons and he laughed in delight as he logged up another high score. He looked so much happier than he had when he'd been admitted and Eve could only hope that social services would sort things out. It wasn't right that a child like this should live in terror.

Evening visiting began a short time later so she went to the office to type up some notes. Ryan always did his own but Rex Manning left it to the F1 students to update the files. Eve never minded doing it as she learned a lot from reading the consultant's observations. She was soon engrossed and didn't hear Penny come into the room. She jumped when the nurse spoke.

'Can you come, Eve? Charlie Lawrence's father is kicking off and I'm not sure what to do,' Penny explained anxiously.

'Of course.' Eve stood up. 'What happened, do you know?'

'I'm not sure but he was in a very belligerent mood when he arrived.' Penny pushed open the door and nodded towards Charlie's bed. 'See what I mean?'

Eve frowned. Even from where she was standing she could tell that Brian Lawrence was in a foul temper. He was glaring down at Charlie's mother, who was cowering in a chair. Charlie was huddled beneath the bedclothes, trying to make himself as inconspicuous as possible. It had all the makings of a major scene and she knew that she had to take immediate steps to control the situation.

'Can you phone Security and ask them to send someone up here as quickly as possible?' she said to Penny. 'I'll go and see if I can calm things down until they arrive.'

'Be careful,' Penny warned her. 'He's a really nasty piece of work and I'd hate you to get on the wrong side of him.'

'I'll be fine,' Eve assured her, although her stomach was fluttering with nerves. She'd been involved in too many similar incidents for it not to have an effect but she refused to let that deter her. There was no way that she was prepared to allow the man to terrorise his wife and child this way.

Amy Lawrence looked round in relief when Eve appeared and she smiled reassuringly at her. 'Hello, Mrs Lawrence. Has Charlie shown you the game he's been playing? He's really good at it.'

'Yes, he did.' Amy Lawrence dredged up a smile. 'He loves those computer games.'

'Most kids do,' Eve agreed. She glanced at Brian Lawrence, who was still looming over his wife. 'Why don't you sit down, Mr Lawrence? I'm sure Charlie would feel a lot happier if you tried to calm down.'

'I don't need advice from the likes of you,' Brian Lawrence snarled. He took a step towards her and Eve had to force herself not to back away. She knew that if she showed even a trace of fear, the situation could spiral out of control. She could see other parents turning to watch what was happening and could only pray that Security would arrive soon.

'Maybe not but you will either have to calm down or leave. I won't have you upsetting the children.'

'I'll do exactly what I choose.' He moved closer, bending so that his face was just inches from hers. 'It's people like you who cause all the trouble, busybodies who poke their noses in where they're not wanted.'

He jabbed a finger into her chest. 'It's you lot who've got social services involved. They came round to the house today, asking all sorts of questions. What I do in my own home is my business, nobody else's, and I told them that before I threw them out. They then had the cheek to tell me they'd be coming back but with the police next time. I won't stand for it, do you hear me? You'll regret calling them in. I'll make sure you do!'

Before Eve could say anything, he grabbed hold of her arm, pushed her into the glass-fronted nurses' station and slammed the door. Eve felt a wave of fear wash over her because it was obvious that he was completely out of control. She backed away, putting the width of the desk between them as she ran through her options, which were all too few. If she tried to force her way out, he would probably retaliate with violence. However, if she tried to stay calm there was a chance that he would calm down too. All she had to do was not antagonise him until Security arrived.

It sounded simple in theory but Eve knew that it wasn't nearly as straightforward as it appeared. There were no certainties when dealing with a man like Lawrence. As she knew to her cost, it would take very little for the situation to escalate.

All of a sudden she wished that Ryan was there. Ryan would know what to do; he'd be able to handle the situation. But Ryan wasn't there. He was out on a date and she was on her own.

Ryan was scrambling some eggs for his supper when the phone rang and he sighed. How typical that the minute he tried to make himself something to eat, he was interrupted. Picking up the receiver, he jammed it between his shoulder and his ear as he continued to stir the eggs. 'Sullivan.'

'Ryan, it's Penny. I'm sorry to phone you at home but we have a major problem on our hands.'

'Why, what's happened?' He scooped the eggs onto a slice of toast and took the plate over to the table.

'Brian Lawrence has shut himself in the nurses' station. Security's here but they've had no luck persuading him to come out.' Penny took a deep breath. 'That's not the worst of it, though. He's got Eve with him and he's refusing to let her go.'

'What?' Ryan exclaimed. He sat down abruptly

as all the strength went out of his legs. 'Tell me what happened right from the beginning.'

He listened with mounting horror as Penny filled him in, barely able to believe what he was hearing. His heart was pounding when she came to the end, the blood rushing through his veins as he thought about Eve being in danger. He couldn't bear it if anything happened to her. He really couldn't bear it!

'I'm coming in,' he told Penny tersely. 'Has anyone called the police? If not, you need to phone them immediately. I'll give Rex a call, too. We may need to evacuate the children so he can sort that out.'

He cut the connection and phoned Rex Manning, briefly explaining what had happened. Rex immediately offered to phone Roger Hopkins, the hospital's manager, which saved Ryan having to do it.

Five minutes later he was in his car and heading to the hospital. He gripped the steering-wheel, sending up a silent prayer that Eve would be all right, but he knew how scared she must be after everything she'd been through in the past.

If only he'd hung around to explain that he'd been lying about his supposed date, none of this might have happened, he thought, and that was the worst thing of all, to know that he could have prevented it if he'd not been such an idiot. He wasn't interested in other women. He was only interested in Eve. And by heaven he was going to make sure she understood that!

CHAPTER FIFTEEN

'THIS WON'T ACHIEVE anything, Mr Lawrence. In fact, you'll only make the situation even more difficult for yourself.'

Eve tried to keep the tremor out of her voice but it wasn't easy. They'd been holed up in the nurses' station for almost an hour and Brian Lawrence wasn't showing any signs of giving up. He was pacing the floor, pausing every few seconds to glare at the small crowd gathered outside. Penny and Tamsin had started to clear the ward and the sound of beds being trundled across the floor provided a constant background noise.

'Shut up!' Lawrence turned and glared at her. 'This is all your fault. If you hadn't got social services involved, none of this would have happened!'

Eve almost laughed out loud. It was so typical of a man like Lawrence to blame everyone else rather than himself. She managed not to react, however, aware that it would take very little to trigger a violent response. She gave a little shrug. 'You'll be able to give your side of the story when the social workers interview you.'

'Why should I have to explain myself to them?' he

snarled. 'How I treat my own child is my business. It's got nothing to do with them or anyone else.'

Eve forbore to say anything, knowing that anything she did say would only antagonise him. She stared through the glass, watching what was going on. Most of the beds had been moved now. There were just a couple left and they would be shifted very soon, she guessed. It was a major disruption and she knew there'd be an investigation into what had happened.

Could she have handled things better if she hadn't been so wound up about Ryan and this date he had? She sighed, uncomfortable with the thought that she might have allowed her emotions to affect her judgement. She had to accept that Ryan wasn't interested in her, not as she wanted him to be.

As though thinking about him had conjured him up, he suddenly appeared. Eve gasped when she saw him stride into the ward. Rex Manning was with him and they both looked very sombre as they approached the nurses' station.

'Mr Lawrence, I have to inform you that the police have been called,' Ryan announced. 'It will be a lot easier for you if you come out of there before they arrive.'

'I'll come out when I'm good and ready,' Brian Lawrence snapped. He swung round so fast that Eve had no chance to evade him as he dragged her out of the chair and propelled her closer to the glass. 'If you try to force your way in here, she'll be the one who suffers.'

'Threatening Dr Pascoe will only make the situation worse for yourself.' Ryan's voice was like steel but

Eve heard the underlying fear it held and felt warmed to the core. He cared about her, he really did, and that made her feel so much better. 'Let her go and I'll make sure the police know that you were willing to co-operate. It will go in your favour.'

'Oh, yes?' Lawrence laughed scornfully. 'Pull the other one, Doc. We both know the police will throw the book at me, which is why I have no intention of letting her go. Dr Pascoe is going to help me get out of here... Oh, and you may as well know that I intend to take my son with me when I leave.'

He reached for the cord on the Venetian blind and lowered it before letting her go. Eve bit her lip as she went and sat down. She had no idea what Lawrence was planning but clearly he wasn't going to release her. She took a deep breath, forcing herself to calm down. She had to sit this out and hope that he saw sense eventually. Her heart lifted. At least Ryan was here and she knew that he would do all he could to get her out safely.

Ryan could barely contain his fear as he explained to the police officer what had happened. Eve was in danger and all he could think about was getting her out. The officer went to confer with his colleagues and Ryan had to stop himself calling him back and demanding to know what he intended to do. Obviously, the police needed to work out a plan, one that would ensure Eve's safety. If that was possible.

His heart contracted as he turned to Rex Manning. 'There must be something we can do to get Eve out of there.'

'I wish there was but you heard what Lawrence said.' Rex shook his head. 'If we try anything, Eve could get hurt. We're going to have to leave it to the police and hope they can make him see sense.'

Rex moved away to speak to Roger Hopkins. Ryan turned to Penny. 'How are the children? Did you manage to find room for them all?'

'Just.' Penny sighed. 'We had to scatter them around the hospital, wherever there was space. It isn't ideal but it's the best we can do.'

'How are Charlie and his mother? Did you put them in PDHU, as I suggested?'

'Yes. Charlie's very quiet but he seems OK. His mum's more upset, in fact. I'll take her a cup of tea and see if that will calm her down.'

'Good idea,' Ryan agreed. 'I'll go and have a word with her while you make it.'

He left the ward and headed to the high dependency unit. There was a policewoman stationed outside the door but she allowed him to pass after he showed her his identity badge.

'What's happening?' Mrs Lawrence demanded when he went into the room. 'Is that young lady doctor still in there with him?'

'I'm afraid so.' Ryan beckoned her over to the door so that Charlie couldn't overhear what they were saying. 'Your husband is refusing to let her go. He intends to use her as a bargaining tool so that he's allowed to leave. Apparently, he plans to take Charlie with him too.'

'No!' Amy Lawrence's face turned ashen. 'You

can't let him take Charlie. Who knows what he'll do to him.'

'Was your husband responsible for the injury to his leg?' Ryan asked quietly.

'Yes. That and umpteen other injuries.' Amy Lawrence's face crumpled. 'I should have left him when he first started hitting Charlie. He kept promising that he wouldn't do it again but he never kept his word. If Charlie did anything to upset him, he'd lash out.'

'Does he hit you too?'

'No. It's only ever Charlie. He's jealous, you see, thinks that because I love Charlie, I don't love him. It wasn't as bad when Charlie was a baby. I used to put him in his cot when Brian got into one of his moods. But now that Charlie's getting older, it isn't possible. I'm on pins every time Brian comes home from work in case Charlie does something to upset him.'

Ryan sighed. It was impossible to understand that kind of attitude. If he had a child, he would love it unreservedly and know that Eve would love it just as much. The thought caught him unawares. It was the first time that he had ever considered having a child, considered it as a possibility, not as something to avoid. His heart was racing as he excused himself. For all these years he had ruled out the idea but now it didn't seem so impossible.

If he and Eve had a child they would love it no matter what. They would work together to ensure that even if their son or their daughter did inherit LQTS, he or she would have a long and happy life. After all, there were drugs available to control the condition, weren't there? His cousins were managing very well on their regimes.

Ryan's head was reeling as he went back to the ward. It was as though every single objection he'd had about having a family had melted away. He could have it all, he realised in amazement, the happy marriage, the kids, everything he'd always believed he had to deny himself…as long as Eve was willing to take the risk.

His heart sank because only Eve could make that decision.

Nine o'clock came and went and they were no closer to resolving the situation. Eve's head was throbbing from all the tension. She closed her eyes, blotting out the flickering glow from the strip lighting. Brian Lawrence had stopped pacing and was standing by the door. She had no idea what he intended to do and didn't bother asking. It was enough that he seemed to have calmed down at last.

'I need to get out of here!' he suddenly exploded, and her eyes flew open.

'Does that mean you're going to give yourself up?' she asked, trying not to show how relieved she felt that the end might be in sight.

'No, it doesn't.' He came over to the desk and dragged her to her feet. 'It means I'm leaving and I'm taking you with me.' He gave a nasty laugh. 'You're going to be my get-out-of jail-free card.'

He clamped his arm around her neck, half dragging and half carrying her to the door. Eve tried to free herself but soon realised how pointless it was when his arm tightened. Flinging open the door, he glared at the people waiting outside. Eve could see several police officers as well as Roger Hopkins and Rex Manning. However, she couldn't see any sign of Ryan and her heart sank. Had he left? Gone back to his date perhaps? The thought that he hadn't cared enough to stay brought tears to her eyes.

'If anyone tries to stop me, she'll be the one who suffers,' Brian Lawrence announced. One of the police officers stepped forward but Lawrence shook his head. 'Forget it. I'm leaving and I'm taking her and Charlie with me.' He looked around the empty ward, only seeming to realise then that the children were no longer there. 'Where is he?'

'Your son is perfectly safe,' Rex Manning assured him. 'If you let Dr Pascoe go, I shall take you to see him.'

Brian Lawrence laughed scornfully. 'Do you think I'm a complete idiot? If I let her go, that's it.' His grip tightened and Eve gasped as her air supply was cut off. 'You'd better tell me where he is and quick if you don't want her getting hurt.'

'He's in the high dependency unit,' one of the policemen said hurriedly.

Eve sucked in a lungful of air as Lawrence's grip slackened. There were black dots dancing before her eyes and her throat felt bruised. It was hard not to show how scared she felt as he dragged her to the door. He obviously knew the layout of the department because he immediately turned right. Out of the corner of her eye Eve saw a flash of movement and then the next moment she was sent sprawling across the floor. Dazed, she stared in amazement at Ryan, who was grappling with Lawrence. There was a short scuffle before the police appeared, a couple of officers quickly subduing the man.

Ryan dropped to his knees beside her. 'Are you all right?'

'I...' It might have been shock, but Eve couldn't seem to get any words out and she saw his eyes darken in concern.

'Eve, darling, talk to me!' He cupped her cheek and she could feel his hand trembling. 'I just need to know that you're all right.'

Eve felt a wave of relief wash over her, not just because she'd escaped from Lawrence but because it was clear how wrong she had been. Ryan did care about her. More than cared. He loved her.

'I'm fine,' she said huskily. Tears slid down her cheeks but they were tears of joy and she smiled through them. 'I'm absolutely fine now.'

He obviously understood what she was saying. Pulling her into his arms, he held her close, held her as though he would never let her go, which was what she wanted more than anything. She stared into his eyes, oblivious to the fact that they had an audience.

'I love you, Ryan. And no matter what problems we face, I shall always love you.'

'I love you too.'

He kissed her then, his mouth telling her everything she needed to hear. Maybe they would have to compromise and she might need to think again about having a family. But she knew that she could do it as long as he was there beside her. He meant the world to her and she couldn't bear to lose him.

The kiss might have lasted even longer than it did. However, a discreet cough finally brought them back to earth. Ryan laughed as he helped her to her feet. 'I think this is one of those scenes that should have *To be continued* tagged onto it.'

Eve chuckled. 'Sounds good to me.'

One of the police officers came over at that point and told her that he needed to take a statement from her. They went into the office while Eve explained what had happened. Once that was done, Roger Hopkins also wanted to know what had gone on so she went over it all again. By the time she'd finished, she was worn out but she still had to finish her shift. She sighed as she stood up. She wanted nothing more than to go home and sleep.

'Right. It's all sorted.' Ryan suddenly appeared. He grinned at her. 'Off you go. I'm going to stay here while you go home.'

'Oh, but I can't let you do that,' she began, but he stopped her in the most effective way possible. Eve sighed as his lips claimed hers. She could get used to being ordered around in this fashion!

He drew back and looked at her. 'You've been through a horrible ordeal tonight, Eve, and you need to go home and rest.' He brushed her bottom lip with his thumb and she shuddered.

'It doesn't seem fair that you should have to work, though,' she protested.

'It isn't a problem and if I'm honest you'll be

doing me a favour,' he countered, his voice sounding very deep.

'How come?' she said huskily, because it was hard not to respond when he looked at her this way.

'Because I'll only worry about you if you insist on working. If I know you're safely tucked up in your bed it will be much easier.'

'In that case, I suppose I don't really have a choice.' She smiled up at him, surprised by how confident she felt all of a sudden. It was as though all the uncertainties had melted away and she felt sure about what she was doing, knew it was what she wanted, knew it was what Ryan wanted too. 'All right, I'll go home on one condition.'

'And that is?'

'That you come and join me after you finish here.'

Sunlight streamed through the bedroom window, casting a golden glow over Eve's skin. Ryan lay on his side, watching as his hand traced the soft curves of her body. He had driven straight to her flat after he'd finished work, using the key she had left beneath the doormat to let himself in. He'd expected her to be asleep but when he had gone into the bedroom she had been waiting for him. Their lovemaking had been quick and urgent, but none the less profound because of that. They both knew how close they'd come to losing each other and relief had added an extra dimension as they had reaffirmed their love.

Now, in the aftermath of their lovemaking, he needed to make sure that Eve understood what it could mean if they stayed together. His heart jolted painfully at the thought.

'I love you.'

Her voice was soft and he shivered when he heard the love it held. That she should love him this much filled him with fear. Was it fair to expect her to face the uncertainty of possibly having a child with a life-threatening condition? Was it right to accept her love and use it to his advantage? What if a time came when she *regretted* falling in love with him: how would it affect her then? She'd been through so much and what she didn't need was more heartache…

'You're doing it again, Ryan. Over-thinking the problem.' She laid her hand against his cheek. 'I love you and because I love you I'm willing to face whatever the future has in store for us.'

'Even if it means us having a child who's affected by LQTS?' he said gruffly, because it was impossible not to feel afraid, not to feel as though he was in the wrong.

'Yes, even that.' Her eyes held his fast. 'I love you and I shall love our child too. I hope he or she won't be affected but if it is we shall deal with it. Together.'

He wanted to believe her so much but years of uncertainty couldn't be ignored. 'Are you sure you can handle the strain, Eve? I know what my parents went through. Even though they were assured that I wasn't at risk, they constantly worried about me. I can't bear to think of you having to go through all that, my love.'

'It wouldn't be easy but I'd cope. I can cope with anything as long as we're together. If that's what you want, of course?'

Ryan frowned. 'Of course it's what I want. I can't think of anything I want more, in fact.'

'Are you sure? I know how wary you've always been of making a commitment and I'd hate to think that you...well, that you've been *backed* into a corner.' She bit her lip. 'I mean, you're already seeing someone else, so it would be better if you told me if you aren't completely sure this is what you want.'

'Oh, I'm sure all right.' He laughed as he hauled her into his arms and kissed her until they were both breathless. He drew back and looked deep into her eyes so there could be no mistake about what he was saying. 'I'm not seeing anyone else, Eve. What I told Marie was a complete and utter fabrication. I simply couldn't admit that my heart was breaking because we'd split up.'

'Oh!'

'Oh, indeed.' He dropped another kiss on her lips, feeling the tension ooze out of her. His hand skimmed down her back, following the line of her spine as he felt desire surge through him once more. It made no difference that they had made love already; he wanted her again!

They made love slowly with a depth and intensity that brought tears to both their eyes. Eve sighed as she snuggled into his arms afterwards. Being with Ryan made her feel complete. It was as though she had rediscovered herself, found the person who had been missing for so long. She knew she had made the right decision, knew that she would never regret it either. She could face anything so long as Ryan was at her side, loving her too.

'I love you,' she said softly. 'I know you're worried but there's no need. I know what I'm doing, Ryan. For the first time in years I know that I can cope with whatever life throws at me.'

'You're sure, aren't you?' he said wonderingly, and she laughed.

'Yes. The old Eve is back, the one who always knew what she wanted.' She dropped a kiss on his lips and grinned at him. 'And what I want is you!'

Five years later

'No! Put that down... Oh!'

Eve gasped as the twins turned the hose on her, soaking her to the skin. She made a lunge for them but they had already taken to their heels and disappeared down the garden. She shook her head, trying not to laugh because it wouldn't send out the right message. Three-year-old Adam and Liam were a pair of little rips, never happier than when they were getting up to mischief. She'd only left the hose unattended for a couple of minutes and now look at the state of her.

'Hmm, either you decided to take a shower or the boys got you.'

Ryan didn't attempt to hide his amusement as he came out of the house. He pulled her into his arms and kissed her, uncaring that her wet clothes were soaking the front of him. He'd been as thrilled as she'd been when tests had proved that neither of the boys had inherited the gene that caused LQTS. Eve knew how worried he'd been, especially after they'd discovered she was having twins, but there'd been no need. Adam and Liam were two healthy and happy little boys, even if they did have a penchant for getting into trouble!

'Your sons are little monsters!' she declared when he let her go.

'My sons?' His right brow arched. 'How come they're mine when they're naughty and yours the rest of the time?'

'That's just how it is,' she said loftily, then squealed when he swung her up in his arms and carried her over to the paddling pool, which she'd been in the process of filling.

'Don't you dare, Ryan Sullivan,' she ordered as he dangled her over the water. 'Ryan, no!'

Cold water sloshed over her as he deposited her in the pool and she gasped. Scrambling to her feet, she stared down at herself for a second then picked up a yellow plastic bucket. 'You're going to regret that,' she warned him, scooping up a bucketful of water.

He tried to sidestep but she was too quick for him. Eve laughed when the water caught him squarely in the chest. 'That should cool you down!' she crowed, refilling the bucket.

Another dousing of cold water ensued before he retaliated by picking up the hose. Eve leapt out of the pool and fled towards the house, laughing when he caught up with her. 'Enough! I'm soaked, you're soaked, so let's call it quits.'

'Good job I'm feeling generous,' he said, grinning at her. He dropped the hose onto the grass then turned her into his arms and kissed her. 'Do you know how much I love you, Eve Sullivan?'

'Enough to stop soaking me with that hose?'

'Yep. That's how much,' he growled, his mouth finding hers again.

Eve closed her eyes and sighed. She hadn't believed that life could be this good but it just seemed to get better every day. She had Ryan and their beautiful boys as well as a job she loved. She had everything she had ever dreamed of and the best thing was that she had found herself too. Wrapping her arms around his neck, she kissed him back. She was the luckiest woman in the world!

* * * * *

A sneaky peek at next month…

MEDICAL ROMANCE

THE ULTIMATE IN ROMANTIC MEDICAL DRAMA

My wish list for next month's titles…

In stores from 7th February 2014:

❏ Tempted by Dr Morales

& The Accidental Romeo – Carol Marinelli

❏ The Honourable Army Doc – Emily Forbes

& A Doctor to Remember – Joanna Neil

❏ Melting the Ice Queen's Heart – Amy Ruttan

& Resisting Her Ex's Touch – Amber McKenzie

Available at WHSmith, Tesco, Asda, Eason, Amazon and Apple

Just can't wait?

Work hard, play harder...

Welcome to the Gold Coast, where hearts are broken as quickly as they are healed. Featuring some of the rising stars of the medical world, this new four-book series dives headfirst into Surfer's Paradise.

Available as a bundle at
www.millsandboon.co.uk/medical